CROSSROADS

CROSSROADS

VINCENT EDMONDS

CROSSROADS

iUniverse books may be ordered through booksellers or by contacting:

iUniverse
1663 Liberty Drive
Bloomington, IN 47403
www.iuniverse.com
1-800-Authors (1-800-288-4677)

Because of the dynamic nature of the Internet, any web addresses or links contained in this book may have changed since publication and may no longer be valid. The views expressed in this work are solely those of the author and do not necessarily reflect the views of the publisher, and the publisher hereby disclaims any responsibility for them.

Any people depicted in stock imagery provided by Thinkstock are models, and such images are being used for illustrative purposes only. Certain stock imagery © Thinkstock.

ISBN: 978-1-5320-3121-2 (sc)
ISBN: 978-1-5320-3122-9 (e)

Library of Congress Control Number: 2017913261

Print information available on the last page.

iUniverse rev. date: 10/25/2017

THIS NOVEL IS dedicated the story tellers in my family, first and foremost to my great, great grandmother Martha Riley whom I never had the pleasure of meeting in person but I learned a great deal about through the many stories passed from one generation to the next, those she narrated along with those chronicled in tales by others.. I would also like mention my great grandmother Leanna Webb and my grandmother Laura Webb each of whom carried the torch keeping the flames of tales alive. Mostly, I would like to give thanks to my mother, Lottie Ford- Edmonds, no matter how many times I didn't believe in my own abilities she pushed me past dark periods in my life, confident, if I believed in myself nothing will be able to prevent me from making my dreams come true. I would also like to thank my sisters Rondya and Renee Edmonds, who have and continue to be my muse, inspiring me with mere smiles, laughter and friendship only siblings can provide. Appreciation is extended to my Wife Denise Edmonds, who has been as eager and desperate as myself to see the pages of my novel make its journey from start to finish, her belief in my efforts and dreams along with her diligent guard against an ever present writers block, her energy and presence chipping away those barriers which threatened to halt progress. I would also like to thank my father Justin Edmonds for introducing me the creative world of arts which sparked my imagination. I would also like to extend special homage to Uncle Richard Riley, Grandpa Bill Edmonds Grandma Helen Hackett- Edmonds, Aunt "Baby" Helen, and all of those lifelong family and friends of 118 North Root Street in Aurora Illinois, who filled my life with imagination, friendship and joy.

This is for you mom, the Crossroads sometimes brings you home.

"People think depression is sadness, crying, or dressing in black. But people are wrong. Depression is the constant feeling of being numb. You wake in the morning just to go back to bed again."

"I keep so much pain inside myself. I grasp my anger and loneliness and hold it to my chest. It has changed me into something I never meant to be. It has transformed me into a person I do not recognize. But I don't know how."

"My biggest fear is that eventually you'll see me the way I see myself."

PROLOGUE

WAS TEN YEARS old when I realized I'd never be a jock. I didn't spend my free hours trying to sculpt my body. I knew that no matter how many barbells I lifted overhead or laps I ran around a track, I'd never transform my small frame into the behemoth I needed to become in order to be successful at winning hard-fought battles on fields where modern-day gladiators warred with one another. I decided instead to focus my time and attention on becoming the next Miles Davis, Dizzy Gillespie or Louis Armstrong.

In the beginning, before I learned how to control my breathing and air placement, my playing of the horn sounded like a man in his last hours of agony after realizing he'd lost his wealth and health and would soon lose his life. Mama sent me to the fields to practice because it was the only place far enough away from human ears. My playing seemed to bother people more than the sounds that Mr. Adams, my fourth grade teacher, made when he raked his fingernails down the chalkboard.

I didn't feel in any way insulted by my mother's request. I carried one of the two remaining chairs from a set of six that had been a part of the old dining room set; I'd been a baby when the wood weathered and the old set began to crumble. Mama had said it belonged to her great-grandmother, and that was the reason she'd not parted with the two remaining chairs. Mama didn't seem sentimental, and she never spoke of her own past. When I asked her how it had been when she was a little girl, she'd look far off into the distance, like her eyes were focused on something beyond the present. I'd ask more about the dining room set, the chairs, and my great-great-grandmother, but Mama lowered her head and concentrated on whatever chore or entertainment that held her attention. Then she'd say in a sullen, soft voice, "Boy, you ask too many questions."

I'd completely stopped asking Mama about the past—or, for that matter, most anything more than the "can I" that children use as their constant verbal barrage similar to the nagging that men accuse women of doing. "Mama, can I go outside? Mama, can I have some more pie? Mama, can I have a new baseball bat?" If I could have written all my school papers on the subject of the can-I, I would've been the next James Baldwin or August Wilson.

For the last real question I asked my mother that had nothing to do with my desire to have or to do something, the inquiry had been about the whereabouts of my father. My mother's expressions went from shock to sullen to placid, and lastly to anger. She metamorphosed before my eyes, her shifting visages from my mother to other faces. These were strange and horrifying transformations that frightened me, much like after I'd stayed up late watching an old black-and-white movie where a regular fella had been bitten by a wolf—but not just any natural moon howler that would make you so scared you'd soil your boxers. The creature that had bitten the fella in the black-and-white movie hadn't been a natural kind of beast; like the gray wolf, it had those qualities that make the wolf a feared and dangerous predator. There had been a purposeful evil, a desire to kill and destroy, that an ordinary wolf doesn't possess. The thing that had bitten the fella hadn't killed him, although I was sure it had wanted to. Instead, the werewolf had bitten the fella, passing the evil and hate and murderous desires that only a man within the beast can possess. It had passed its curse into the fella, who later transformed from a regular guy into a hideous monster. My mother's transformation when I'd asked her about my father had reminded me of that movie where the fella had been cursed and transformed into a monster. I then decided that I'd never ask Mama about Daddy—or, for that matter, anything else.

When my mother demanded that I practice my horn in the fields, I knew standing for hours would leave me with sore feet and tired legs. That was when I got the idea to use one of the chairs that survived from the old set. I had a bit of trepidation about whether I should ask my mother about borrowing one of the two remaining dining room chairs. I'd make sure to phrase my request in the can-I format. I knew that although Mama wouldn't speak of it, it held memories for her. I'd learned when Mama was forced to look back over the years, if there was too much pain or hurt, she'd transform into something I never wanted to see. I thought about simply taking the chair, carrying it into the cotton field so I'd have a place to sit while practicing my trumpet far from the sensitive ears of human life. But Mama might get upset over my taking it without asking. Then I wouldn't need a chair to sit in, because my backside would be so sore that I wouldn't be able to sit on my bum for days without being reminded by the sting I'd feel on my cheeks. Instead of taking the chair, I'd ask if I could.

"Mama, can I use Gr …?" I decided to leave Great-Great-Grandmother out of the equation altogether. She wasn't among the living any longer, and as Mama said, the dead didn't have a say in things anymore. "Mama, can I use the dining room chair to sit on while I practice my trumpet in the field?" I asked instead.

Mama paused and didn't respond for a few seconds. Like the cat had her tongue. Then she smiled her crooked smile, where on one side of her mouth (usually her left side) turned up. That was as much of a smile as Hattie Blackman could muster. "Yes, Leroy, you can borrow it. But if one of the legs or the back falls apart, you make sure you fix it. You hear me?"

"Yes, Mama," I responded, thankful for the chair and the fact that my request hadn't stirred the beast within from its slumber.

The trumpet was my escape from that black cloud that hovered above the heads of the poor and misfortunate and poured rain down on only them, like those doomsday clouds that dropped rain on the poor cartoon characters that couldn't seem to buy good luck; misfortune followed them wherever they went. Practicing my trumpet and getting past an inability to produce a spitting, sputtering sound like a baby made when discovering an ability to produce noises with his mouth was the closest I came to duplicating the trumpet. But slowly over time, with practice, I was producing sounds that mimicked the beginning of what would later become music. There was the possibility of being good at something, and even being admired and respected, because in spite of all my lacking, I was talented. The trumpet represented the hope that was Everest in the mind of a child, where peaks were looked upon and reached for without fear of falling.

I thought of the trumpet like it was a companion; it had been my friend in times of loneliness. When you're an only child without a father, and with a mother who cannot reach beyond her own demons and is prevented from loving in a functional manner, you learn to befriend life-forms of lesser needs and desires. Human wants sour or wane over time because of all the giving and taking. Mostly it's because of the taking. I'd made friends with toys, plastic cowboy and Indian miniatures molded to resemble images of living frontiersmen and Native Americans. They were playthings I eventually became bored of because I'd reached the limits of my imagination in adventures to take them on or, as had been in most cases, I'd out grown my childhood inclinations. There had been dogs, cats, and even a raccoon who visited my back porch; eventually we gained enough trust in one another that I fed the raccoon by hand. But even with my pets, much as I loved and gave to them of my energies, they couldn't return it because of their inability to have a relationship beyond their own natural ability.

In the trumpet and the struggle to play it, to master notes and sounds, I discovered my life's companion, that creature of mind, soul, and body. In my time of hopelessness and being lost in the seeming futility of waking, working, living, and sleeping, there were repetitive behaviors that would not and could not replace the emptiness. I later discovered that this constant and never-ending routine did not move me forward but only managed to allow me to spin in circles, feigning distance and movement but in truth not getting me any closer to knowing myself, God, or my true purpose. The trumpet, in my efforts to master each note, feel every sound, and listen to the notes, spoke to me like the voice of God, a creator that in return didn't judge or blame, that didn't ask that I suffer for naught in this life and have to wait for my treasure in the hereafter. No, this God gave rewards now, giving me my just due for the efforts I provided in life, the instant gratification that a lonely child craved and was deprived of having.

When I was a child in a field, sitting on a dining room chair that had once belonged to my great-great-grandmother, I knew nothing of the woman except that she'd lived and at some point in her life had owned a wooden dining room table and mahogany chairs, each with tan cushions to soften the space between someone's rear end and the hard surface of the stained wood. Perhaps my mother kept the two remaining chairs as a reminder to her of a woman who in some way, for good or bad—most likely good, or so I'd like to believe—had left an impression upon her.

I was surrounded by soft white plums of cotton stalks that sometimes towered over me, their bud-heavy tops leaning in close as if to whisper some unknown secret only in the last minute before releasing their hidden words. They reared upward and leaned in a direction opposite of where I was seated. The cotton stalks bobbed and weaved in the wind like the heads and bodies of men and women in juke houses that I'd later perform in during my adult life, after forgetting how I'd fallen in love and befriended my trumpet. It replaced the innocent admiration and friendship with senseless desires of riches and fame that it seemed all men, once driven of purpose and hope, succumbed to. Men lost themselves in the lust of their wants and cravings, hungers that could never be sated no matter how much was consumed, because lust and desire were ravenous and had stomachs that were as vast and endless as space. I had forgotten about the solitude, the bonds and struggles, and the victories. How sweet and magnificent they had been when I finally found cohesion in lungs, air, lips, and breaths that in some miraculous way conceived the birth of my ability to produce sounds and tones that could have caused spirits of men to rise above earthly chains, breaking the grip of their despondencies.

But no. Instead, I chose to ignore a greater purpose—perhaps what those bud-laden cotton stalks had been trying to whisper and warn me not to do. I chose a lesser format of perfecting my art. I parlayed with men and women dirty in thoughts and energies. And for what? I traded purpose and soul in order to have riches and fame—nothing of real worth.

I recall every finite detail, so much so I can almost taste, smell, and hear the memories. I remember that the dullness of my hangover has been push away, and damn, I remember. The only thing I want to do is reach for the bottle—whisky, bourbon, or the moonshine. I'd like to blame the booze for my stupidity, but in truth, the intoxicating brew is not the master of this wayward ship. But I'd like to drink right about now, until drunkenness steals memories and accountability.

Leroy Blackman

Part One

THE BEGINNING OF THE END

LEROY'S BLUES

1.

WOULD YOU SELL your soul for it? Well, would you?

Leroy Blackman had been asked this question in his nightmare. The night terror had awakened him, with images of his dream still visible and fresh in his mind. His nightmare felt real more than an illusion caused by an overactive subconscious. He'd not answered the question, at least not before being awakened by fears associated with such an inquiry. It required more thought before answering with a simple yes or no. In the question, he'd been asked if he'd sell his soul for it—the forbidden delving into his hidden musing. The consideration of selling his soul had been tossed back and forth in his mind as he weighed the cons and pros for whichever choice he made. For most people who may consider such a bargain, what answer they'd give had to do with how deeply was their desire to have the empty spaces in their lives filled with whatever it was that could replace the void, which was deepened and widened by loss or time. They did not discern what it was that experience and age matured. It was an ability to know and to make better decisions about what they'd sacrifice in order to have it.

That knowledge enhanced by foresight that came with duration, would determine how the majority of desperate folks, similar in the despondencies and emotions of dispiritedness causing Leroy Blackman to entertain such an ill-advised trade, would answer. The weight of loss and voracity of desire would determine how they'd answer such a grave question. Leroy knew it could and would mean anything, with no limits except for a lack of imagination. It could be love, riches, fame, fortune, or revenge. For a crippled man, it may be an ability to walk again. For a blind woman, it may be to see a sunrise. For a poor, down-on-his-luck bum whose only possessions were the rags on his body, it may be enough wealth to never have to worry again.

Although Leroy did believe he knew the answer to the question, when he'd been awakened because of fear at seeing the image of the interrogator, who'd stood across from him and asked him that question. "Would you sell your soul for it?" The interrogator had asked while staring into his soul like a predator, like a snake that lured its prey with a hypnotic sway of its long, scaly body until the rat or squirrel fell into a spell-binding trance. The dancing, the back-and-forth movements, were only a seductive ruse to ease trepidations. When the pirouette was finished, flesh and bone, and his soul—it seemed possible, at least in his dreams—would be consumed as substance. The interrogator came forth from Leroy's deepest, darkness fears, a place in the mind where shape and form were given to creatures lying in wait beneath beds or within closets, waiting for lights to dim and the darkness to take dominion. It was the hour and conditions for evil, the witching hour, the time of night when demons or zombies, along with those terrors that only took shape in nightmares, would rise from bottomless pits and have their way with humankind.

After having the dream that didn't feel like a dream, Leroy awoke feeling like he'd been kicked in his head by a mule, knocked silly. The mule, the surly bastard that had knocked him unconscious and was the reason he'd awaken with a throbbing frontal lobe and a monster of a headache, hadn't resembled the four-legged, dull-looking pack animal known for its stubbornness. Leroy had been kicked, but the power punch had come from contents within a clear mason jar that had previously bottled the power of a heavyweight knockout artist. The mason jar had been used to store products such as syrup, pickled cucumbers, or honey. Now, moonshiners favored the mason jar as a means of bottling their product when it was ready for sale and consumption. Juke houses sold homemade whisky and it had been the brew that had caused his eyeballs to roll back into whites of their sockets, leaving him unconscious and unaware of the comings and goings around him, or of the chainsaw sound of his own snoring.

Leroy recalled some events from the previous evening. The majority of that night was a blur of sights, a confused mixture of voices, laughter, and music. He remembered the argument he'd had with Shelly; she'd called him an alcoholic bastard. What a disrespectable thing for a wife to refer to her husband as, he'd thought. She shouldn't have called him that. It didn't matter that it was true. It wasn't something she was supposed to say. Leroy lay in bed, trying to extract from his abashed memoires the details of what had happen after he'd stormed out of the house, dodging the pots and glass drinking cups Shelly threw in his direction with the speed and accuracy of a major league pitcher. Fortunately for his sake, he hadn't had to stand still and wait to see if what she threw in his direction would be a ball or strike; his batter's box included the entire house and extended to the front porch and yard.

"You alcoholic son of bitch!" he heard Shelly scream from behind the screen door he'd slammed in her face after he'd opened it and ran out on to the front yard. He'd quickly opened the driver's side door of his Oldsmobile fumbled with his key, having as much trouble inserting the key into the ignition as a virgin did trying to find the correct angle to enter a woman's treasure box. He'd managed to get the car started, placed it in reverse, and backed out of the dirt driveway and onto the gravel road. He'd paused on the road parallel to his front door, and he saw Shelly's face, a scrawl of anger and frustration that disfigured her beauty. He released his grip on the steering wheel with the hand closest to the driver's side window, and he folded all his fingers into his palm except one. Then with his free hand, he rolled down the window. As he did, he stuck out the hand that was giving Shelly the bird. He allowed his middle finger to pause long enough to provide the effect he desired. He could see Shelly's mouth begin to open, no doubt to scream curses in his direction, but he'd hit the gas before her words traveled from the porch to his ears. Rocks and dirt spewed from beneath his rear tires, and a cloud of dust billowed upward behind the ass of his Olds. His finger allowed him the last word in their argument, and he smiled as he sped along the dirt road.

He made a left on an unnamed path about five miles west of his home. The back road was in even worse condition than the gravel road on which he'd been driving. The Olds rocked and dipped as tires fell into and climbed back out of deep, wide potholes on the unpaved path.

The illegal drinking and gambling establishments were owned by businesspeople who chose not to give Uncle Sam his share of the bounty they collected, or else they'd be forced to walk that ridiculous tightrope that had to be balanced in order to get across the space of bureaucracy that allowed some men to succeed in business while those legal hurdles that had to be cleared prevented others from having their piece of the American pie. Most Southern towns and backwoods, after-hour establishments were referred to as juke houses, because back in the day they'd been places where men and women could juke and jive all night long while they listened to the blues or jazz and drank homemade liquor. For those really brave or foolish souls, they could take their week's earnings to the back room, where dice was rolled and men placed bets on which of them had the best hand of cards. Leroy's poker face couldn't fool an infant, so he stayed clear of the door leading to the back room. He didn't frequent juke houses to gamble; that wasn't his guilty little sin.

Bits and pieces of his memory, which when he'd first been awakened by the nightmare had been like hundreds of scrambled puzzle pieces, were beginning to make sense. It was like when puzzle pieces were placed in the correct location and began to form a picture. He'd driven to Greenwood after arguing and dodging pots pans and glassware. He'd paid for those kitchen items, and the thought pissed him off because Shelly would blame him for having to spend the money to replace the broken dishes. He fast-forwarded past the current thought because it was the less exiting and most obvious part in a movie he'd already watched. He wanted to view the mysterious scene in the movie—the parts writers, directors, and actors steered moviegoers toward at a slow, deliberate pace so that they thought they knew exactly what direction the action was going, only to learn they'd been mentally and emotionally baited and switched. In the movies, especially the ones you've already seen, you fast-forward through the scenes that don't stimulate your senses. The awkward and seemingly thrown-in love stories that producers use to advertise to a female audience and that are not enough to ruin a good action thriller like, say, a James Bond movie. Still, in a better world one dominated by male testosterone and not watered down so much by female energies, entertainment meant for men is thinned so much that masculinity resembles a 150-pound weakling getting sand kicked in his face. Women in full doses, their wanting nagging and complaining, are like succubi draining from men the essence of what it is to be wild, free, and untamed. The energy of women, let loose to roam without restraints, is a ravenous force of nature. Unabated, it will feed, consume, and digest, leaving the world men have labored and fought to create as barren as wastelands where nothing of substance will grow. Women's needs and desires, if too much of them are allowed to spread, can ruin a good movie, much as her constant nagging, complaining, and temperament can stem a man's erection until his pecker turtles up and retreats into the shell of its skin.

Leroy scolded himself for his currents thoughts, because much as he thought he'd fast-forwarded past Shelly's torrent display, her childlike reaction to his God-given right as a grown-ass man, being a man and an adult provided him with certain rights, didn't it? Yes, he believed having made it from childhood to a grown man, it did. Shelly had no right behaving the way she did. Her response had been downright disrespectable, and when he'd fully awakened, he'd get to the business of reminding her why, as a man, he was the one who called the shots.

He tightened his eyes to shield against thoughts of Shelly—and the headache that was pounding at his frontal lobe and temples like a cop banging on a door demanding entrance into his home. He had to get past his thoughts of Shelly. He'd rewind and deal with her later. Right now, he wanted to get past driving to Greenwood, to what happened after. It seemed to him—and he couldn't explain his feelings—but what happened after Greenwood felt bad. Because of the nightmare, the strange, eerie interrogator who had stood on the road in his dream hadn't felt like a dream. And of course there was that question: "Would you sell your soul for it?"

"I lay in bed for hours in the dark at night, thinking about
every possible thing I fucked up in my life."

THE COMPANY I KEEP

THE BACK ROAD was more a unkempt path that was simultaneously cleared and ruined by tires of vehicles that deepened natural sinking holes of earth and loosened the grip of gravel or dirt, so that when there was a heavy downpour, the drenched, loose rocks and earth caused the path to be impassable. The back roads shortened the distance between Inverness and Greenwood, Mississippi, but they were the black holes of the South, where space folded in on itself, and anyone desiring to brave the dangers of flat tires, broken axles, or front-end damage could forgo wasted hours in travelling paved streets to get from one town to the next.

This back road was five miles from Leroy's house—if that plywood-constructed, three-room dwelling with a roof made of sheets of thin metal that couldn't muffle or dam water from passage could be referred to as a home. Leroy attempted to ignore his new thoughts as he had those of his wife, but it was a difficult thing to do because so much of who, why, where, and when of his life has to do with his current living conditions. He tried because if he didn't, he knew he'd never get his mind past Greenwood, which he needed to do in order to answer some of the questions he'd asked himself after he'd awakened with the god-awful pounding in his head, and after having the nightmare that seemed too real to have been an illusion. Questions were buried deep down in the dark recesses of his memories—cancerous questions that, if he didn't quickly answer, would grow in his mind and consume his sanity.

I argued with Shelly, he thought, and this time he didn't allow his mind to linger on Shelly or his feelings about what she'd said or done. *Then I took the back road to Greenwood.* He didn't ponder over thoughts of where he lived or how the road had caused him to bounce up and down in the bucket seat of his Olds like he was on the back of an unbroken bronco. He relaxed his mind like a man sitting alone in a dark movie theater, his hand full of salt, butter, and fluffy popcorn, which he washed down with a large container filled with Coke-neither of which he'd be forced to share, and he wouldn't have to hear complaints about the lack of nutritional value and how, if he wanted popcorn, he should at least ask for a tub without flavored butter or salt. Also, water, not highly sugared and caloric soft drinks, was a better way to quench his thirst—that was, if he must drink while eating, which of course wasn't good for his digestion.

Leroy didn't scold himself for his current mental tangent. His sudden break in meditative thoughts of Shelly seemed to find a way to disturb his inner peace, much in the same way her nagging over his diet ruined his state of mind in a movie theater. Thoughts of Shelly steered him away from his current direction; it had been only a slight veer away from the direction he was going, so he didn't scold himself too much for allowing himself the quick detour

He'd taken the shortcut through the back road to get to Greenwood because he'd gone to Miss Ruby's, which meant it had been Friday night. Miss Ruby's juke joint ran a special on chicken wings, fried chicken legs, and (most important to Leroy) half off on drinks.

The usual suspects who frequented Ruby's had been present last night, give or take a few who hadn't shown. Those new faces didn't look so different from the old faces that they'd replaced. Big Lou had been guarding the front door of Ruby's with all of the focus and detail a grade-school child had minutes before school let out before summer break. Big Lou had to be the worst security guard from Greenwood to Jackson, and that was giving him the benefit of the doubt that others somewhere were worse. Big Lou had greeted him with a big watermelon-eating grin, revealing his yellow-stained choppers and black gums. His big old country ass needed to stop his diet of Kit Kat bars, and his habit of chewing and spitting tobacco needed to be stopped before his gums rotted and all his teeth fell out. "What's up, my man Leroy? You sho is looking good, my brother," Big Lou had said looking Leroy up and down like he was wrapped in a package of his favorite chocolate bar. The rumor was Big Lou had another kind of sweet tooth—one he'd picked up from his five years behind bars at parchment, and he couldn't or didn't want to break it upon his release.

Leroy didn't concern himself with gossip. He didn't care if big Lou had transformed from king of the jungle into queen of the Nile, or if he swung back and forth from both branches. However, he had to admit he didn't appreciate being gawked over by a man like he was exposing hidden desires beneath his outerwear that a man would walk through fires of hell to get to. But Big Lou stood six foot four and had to be near three hundred pounds of mostly muscle. If Lou hemmed him up in some dark corner and rumbled in his deep baritone voice while having that ridiculous watermelon smile painted across his face, "Hey,

Leroy. You know I've always wanted you," then Leroy knew he'd take his best swing at the Goliath doorman. But until that day, like anyone else with brains enough to allow him to walk and talk at the same time, he'd pretend to ignore any strange looks or feelings that were had when Big Lou looked at him in that leering, unmanly way.

"Thanks, Lou. You know I gotta stay fly for the ladies." Leroy emphasized his point by saying *ladies* slowly and more clearly than the rest of his response, hoping his point wasn't lost.

"Well, yeah, there be plenty of fine yellow-boned women inside," Big Lou said. He knew Leroy's personal attraction was toward light-skinned black women, so light their skin complexion was a smooth, yellow blonde color. "You know I like mine dark as coal, like they make in the mother land," Big Lou said as Leroy walked past him and through the front door of Ruby's.

Leroy acted like he didn't get the double meaning behind Big Lou's comment, or notice Lou's eyes staring at his backside. Leroy is dark as night, the complexion of men born in the mother land, and unlike many men his color, Leroy never had a problem with being African black. In fact, his coal-colored skin attracted women to him like pollen drew honey bees to the most colorful flowers. Hearing Big Lou's comment caused him, for the first time in his life, to feel sensitive about his complexion. He shook off Big Lou's comment and his lusting gaze and strolled toward an empty stool at the bar.

Leroy was five feet eight inches in his shoes, and stripped down to his boxers, he weighed about 155 pounds, depending on whether he'd checked his weight before filling his stomach with Shelly's meals, which always added four to five pounds to his walking-around weight. Leroy was a little man in stature, but he'd swear to anyone listening, "I'm herculean where it counts." Then he'd give a smile and a wink. "If you get the meaning to what I'm implying," he'd add. Leroy had learned early on in life that he wasn't going to be an athletic superstar. Classmates taught him that lesson in the fields behind school yards or the abandoned lots, where customers once parked cars before grocery chains or retail stores packed their merchandise and moved them (along with the jobs) to cities where they could make more profit from the items they sold. Fortunately, Leroy didn't have to have the snot knocked out of him or be laughed at because he wasn't born with the hand-eye coordination to hit a white ball with a bat, or to shoot a ball through a net. He'd learned his lesson quickly, and because he had, Leroy hadn't wasted time dreaming of or attempting to become the next Spud Web or Nate "Tiny" Archibald.

Leroy did discover something he could do, and after much practice, he did it very well. Leroy didn't remember the first time he saw or heard a trumpet. He always knew the Archangel Gabriel had chosen the instrument to perfect above all others, and that it was his trumpet that would preclude the beginning of the end of world. But it hadn't been Gabriel's horn that he'd heard or seen that provided him the epiphany, the third-eyed type of wisdom that enlightened men when their thoughts were in darkness. There were those biblical stories of trumpets bringing down walls, and of course Gabriel's earth-rumbling note that announced to sinners and saved alike of Jesus's return. Leroy believed those images resided in his subconscious and played a role, even if only a minor one, in his final decision. He was sure that it was Miles and Dizzy, and before them, Louis Armstrong. Louis had a bright and intoxicating smile, wide eyes, unordinary charm, and the nickname Satchmo. *What a hip bluesman nickname,* Leroy had thought when he'd first heard Louis Armstrong's moniker. Louis Armstrong, along with Miles Davis and Dizzy Gillespie, inspired Leroy to take up the trumpet—not simply to play it, but to be great so that folks with a musical intellect would turn their heads. He wanted to change lives with the sounds emitting from brass-stained horns similar to how the emissions held in the hands of the best three trumpeters who ever placed their lips on stainless-steel mouthpieces, blowing air from their lungs and perhaps their souls. Yes, their souls. Leroy thought that only air from a man's soul could make an inanimate object produce noises that sounded like living voices.

Shelly and Leroy had argued because she'd wanted him to stay home, not spend hours and hard-earned money purchasing intoxications that had been cooked in iron stills deep in the backwoods of Inverness, cooked and brewed until the corn and mixture of moonshiners' secret ingredients boiled to one hundred proof. She'd become angry over Leroy's nonchalance and truculent reactions. She'd thrown dishes and whatever else was within her ability to lift and throw with some amount of accuracy. In the end, he'd left, and even before driving away, he had further disrespected Shelly by giving her the bird. Then he'd driven down the back roads toward Greenwood, and from there he'd driven to Miss Ruby's place, where once he'd passed the door and gotten far away from Big Lou and the curse of Ham that had followed Big Lou as it had Noah's son and Ham's future generations from the cave where Ham had looked upon his own father's nakedness.

Leroy headed straight to the bar, ordered a mason jar of moonshine, and drank it at what might be a moderate speed, which for any drunk was difficult because when one was an alcoholic, the purpose of drinking was simply to get drunk. The Creole girl sitting on a stool two down from his she was fine, with yellow-blonde skin that was smooth as silk. There was not a flaw on her face. She'd squeezed her round, shapely hips and full breasts into a tight pink dress. In truth, a women as attractive as the light-skinned Creole girl could have been dressed in burlap, and every horny gent would have still been attempting to discover what was beneath the animal skin she was wearing.

Leroy played it cool, which was smart because women liked a man with a bit of mystery to him, much as men liked women who didn't go showing all of her goodies, only enough to tease and tempt; that was respectable, enticing. Leroy's "cool as the other side of the pillow" routine must have worked, because before he'd finished his second glass of moonshine, the Creole girl was smiling and batting her long lashes in his direction Leroy ordered another drink, this one for her, and he nodded in her direction, holding up the glass so she'd know his intentions. She sashayed toward him, her hips, ass, and breasts bouncing left and right, up and down. He had to stop trying to take all of her in, because the constant movement of her body was making him dizzy.

"Hey, Dark Chocolate. Is that drink for me?" She'd nicknamed him already, and he liked that. Her voice was soft and sweet, and if a voice could smell or taste, hers would have filled his nose and mouth with the sensations of sweet potato pie. They started up a conversation with the small and obvious talk. "What's your name? Where you from? What brings you to Ruby's?" The talk one had to get out of the way before one could discover if one was going to ride this roller coaster, or save the ticket for a bigger, more exciting ride.

In less than an hour, they'd drank enough for the good feeling to spread from their feet to the tops of their heads. Like most drunks when they'd consumed far too much and still were on their feet, Leroy began to tell more about himself to the Creole girl than what he'd reveal to his closest friends or relatives when sober. She said her name was Lana Monroe. Leroy begin to tell Lana his life story, the good along with the bad. She'd mentioned something about getting back all he lost and more, and she said his life didn't have to be over; he could get a second chance. He laughed, but she didn't. He said, "Well, if you'll show me how to do that trick, turn this fifty-year-old clock in my body back a few years, I'm listening."

She'd explained in detail, and Leroy was nervous, so he laughed. If she'd been an average-looking women and not a sex goodness, he would have gotten away from her crazy ass. Women who talked the way she had about witchcraft and voodoo were meant to be stayed clear of. But Leroy's johnson was stirring in his pants, and she was taking crazy talk. In his head, Leroy knew better than to listen to, but to the brain in his trousers, her crazy words didn't mean anything.

Leroy left Ruby's and watched the entire room full of jealous, envious gents stare at him with jealously as he marched through the door with his head up, and strutting like a peacock with his feathers flaring and his neck bobbing. Leroy had allowed Lana Monroe to provide him with directions to a dark road in the middle of nowhere. There wasn't much about the Delta cities Leroy didn't know or hadn't seen, or at least heard about. She'd taken him to a secret place, an evil, forbidden, cursed place. As the memory of events became clearer, Leroy opened his eyes. *Fuck the headache, the spinning room, the hangover, Shelly's disrespect, my lost youth. Fuck all of it to hell, because that's exactly where I'm going. I remember now,* Leroy thought. *I followed the Creole girl, Lana Monroe, to the crossroads where … Naw, I couldn't have done that. It had to be a dam dream, a nightmare, the kind that seem real when you first awake.* Would you sell your soul, boy? "Would you sell your soul to be really good at playing that horn again? For fame, for wealth, for women—would you, boy?" Leroy thought he'd answered yes, but it was a crazy nightmare, nothing more. He'd turn over to the other side of the bed, to where Shelly slept; he wanted to touch her, feel her skin, smell the sour aroma of her morning breath, and feel the warmth of her body. He was like a child waking from a horrible dream, needing the comfort of his mama in order to set his world straight, because the nightmare had turned him and his beliefs upside down.

Shelly hadn't been there, not lying in her usual right side of the marital bed. Instead of his wife lying next to him, there was Leroy's childhood trumpet. The instrument he'd stop playing, stopped believing in, stopped loving somehow. It had found him, crawled up in bed to him, and snuggled like a mistress he'd forsaken for years. Leroy was excited and terrified, and at the same time, he was overjoyed to see his old friend. He was mortified because of where it had travelled from to find him. "Would you sell your soul, boy?" The eerie voice he'd heard standing at the crossroads, where the crazy Creole Lana Monroe had said she could help him get back all he'd lost and a little more, that it wasn't too late, that she knew a way to help. Leroy was remembering, and he scooted away from his trumpet like it was a snake about to bite him. "What in the hell is going on?" he whispered.

Leroy sat on the edge of his bed, his shoulders hunched and his forearms resting on his thighs. The mornings after the boozing and behaving like an adolescent were punishment for indulging in activities that he knew he shouldn't but chose to ignore. When the fun had been had and the light rose in the eastern sky, it illuminated shadows, revealing the beauty as well as the ugliness. He'd try to run and hide, but there was no place to bury himself from his shame.

"Shelly," Leroy shouted, and he regretted speaking aloud. His voice bounced inside his head like an echo traveling through tunnels of narrow, dark caves. He grunted while riding the waves of pain his own voice has caused. *Where the hell is she?* Leroy thought. He tried to use logic, which was difficult with his skull feeling like a woodpecker was pecking at it from the inside. He stood with one hand on his skull and the other stretched out in front of him, gripping the air for balance. He opened his eyes enough to squint. Walking like an old man with a bad hip and a severe case of arthritis in both his knees, Leroy made his way from the bedroom to the living room.

Like the bedroom, the living room was decorated with cheap, old furniture, and it was absent of Shelly's presence. The kitchen was the final room within the walls of his home; the toilet was one hundred feet from the house, a dug-out hole covered with a box of plywood and the same thin, metal sheets that covered the roof of the house. *If Shelly is sitting on the box, her ass propped up on the plastic toilet cover, then I'll just have to wait until she's finished. The last thing I want to view is her naked ass sitting on the box with her dress hiked up around her thighs while she pees or dumps.* Leroy was thinking about Shelly on the box and also about opening the back door, pushing past the screen, and heading to the three wooden steps that led to the backyard and the outhouse. Standing and walking had shaken his bladder, and now the contents of it were flowing like a rain-swollen river toward the tip of his johnson. Looking through half-opened eyes, Leroy did not see Shelly, and neither did he hear sounds of women's work in the kitchen: the mixture of pots and pans clanging together, water boiling, or bacon sizzling on a frying pan. *Shelly's not in the kitchen either. She must be on the box.*

Leroy couldn't ignore his own need to relieve the building pressure in his bladder. Because Shelly was in the outhouse, and because he didn't feel a need to walk the distance, pissing out of the back door and into the yard was more convenient. *Shelly hates when I haul my johnson out of my trousers, poke it through the zipper of my pants, and pee behind a tree or side of the house or through the open kitchen door into the back yard. Ain't my fault she wasn't born with an ability to piss standing up,* Leroy thought. His zipper was halfway down, and he was already feeling the relief that would come when the faucet was opened and the flow of piss was released. "Damn it," Leroy said as he stumbled. His feet impacted with something on the floor directly on the path between him and the back door, and he stumbled and realized it was the sort of off-balance mishap that he'd not recover from. He would dance for a while and then eventually fall.

The bulky softness that broke his fall, preventing him from impacting with the harder, sturdier wooden floor, felt uncomfortably familiar. He rolled to his butt and backed away from the bulk. Leroy continues backing away until his shoulders were halted by a wall, his feet still pushing back because his mind had not registered that his body was no longer moving. The squint through which he'd been viewing the world was replaced with bug-eyed clarity, no blurred or half images. He could see perfectly now, and what he saw was an utter nightmare.

Shelly hadn't been in the bed next to him. She hadn't been watching the morning news on television in the living room, or fixing breakfast in the kitchen. She wasn't in the outhouse. She wasn't in any of those places because Shelly is lying on the floor between the path from the entrance into the kitchen, and where he'd been on his way to the back door to relieve his bladder. Seeing Shelly lying on the wooden floor, surrounded by red, dry fluid, ignited a few more memories. The Creole girl, the crossroads, a man he couldn't recall much about. The face and image were vacant, like matter that was consumed by a dark hole and was disfigured so much one could no longer determine what the object had once been before being distorted by the crushing weight of the dead star that transformed into invisible, ravenous force that could only be describe as a black hole.

"Would you sell your soul for it, boy?" That had been the question. He'd thought when first remembering the eerie voice in his head that it had all been a dream. Now, seeing Shelly lying on the floor of the kitchen in a puddle of mostly dried blood, he realized none of it had been a dream. He was living in a nightmare, but not a dream, not the terrifying illusions that gripped one's unconscious mind and could only can keep one prisoner while one remain asleep. *I am in a waking nightmare. Shelly is dead.* "Would you sell your soul for it, boy?"

"Yes, I would," he believed he'd said. "I'd sell my soul for the fame, for the fortune, and for the only lover I ever really had, the companion I fell head over heels for, pressing my lips to steel, caressing smooth curves with delicate fingers. I'd sell my soul to play again, in order to feel like I had when I was a ten-year-old kid, sitting in a cotton field on a chair that had once belonged to my great-great-grandmother, discovering the voice of my God. Yes, I'd sell my soul for it."

"We all get addicted to something that takes away the pain."

SHELLY'S BOX

1.

SISSY ABSENTLY REACHES into a container. It's really nothing more than an inexpensive cardboard box, and the contents within were sealed like the way animals came to Noah's ark in pairs, probably all together, including the last two she grabbed and freed from plastic coverings. Together all twelve swiss rolls, which were nothing more than sugar and artificial flavorings. The cardboard box had been designed to lure her. The swiss rolls were flavored to trick the taste buds and provide the stomach with a full yet inadequate amount of substance. The box was probably designed by some big shot in New York who sat behind his desk in an office with a window view of buildings that, like the Tower of Babel, attempted to reach the heavens and would be cast down by God's vengeful justice. The New York businessman probably worked all day, just like Satan and his fallen two hundred, thinking of ways to entice God's children and lead them astray. Satan had deceived Adam and Eve, causing them to sin and then to be cast out of paradise. The men and women who tempted the world called what they did branding, but in truth it wasn't anything more than sinful in purpose and design.

As Sissy sat in her kitchen stuffing the last two swiss rolls into her mouth, she thought if she'd eaten the carefully designed container that had been designed to bait her, she'd probably get more nutritional value from it. The box had at some point been a tree, a living thing. It had been deformed by man's evil intentions, but it had at one point been a creation of God, unlike the swiss rolls.

Gluttony is sinful, she thought. However, she made excuses for overeating, and she attempted to trick herself into believing the sin of gluttony wasn't as bad of a sin—not like the other deadly vises that caused men to lose their souls and be tossed into the pits of hell. Sissy was a nickname since birth. She'd been called that because it seemed Southerners named kids one thing at birth but referred to them by a nickname for the duration of their live. Sissy's official name is Sara Cousin's. It's the name on all of her government documents, her driver's license, her social security card, her credit cards, and the passport she'd sent away for five years ago because she'd plan to travel, but in truth, even when she'd sat in front of the camera and had taken her picture taken for her passport, she'd known she'd never travel outside of the Delta in Mississippi. Sara was a good name, a biblical name, a name she shared in common with the wife of Abraham, who for a brief moment had lost her way when she'd believed her age had taken away her ability to bring life forth from her womb. *God can do all things,* Sissy thought. "Praise God," she whispered as she raised her hands over head and wiggled her chubby, chocolate-streaked fingers toward the heavens. She wasn't going to worry about her overconsumption of food or about the excessive pounds the chocolate bars, swiss rolls, and sugar cookies, just to name a few sinful overindulgences, causes. In God's holy and miraculous hour, he revealed to Abraham's Sara his holy power and gave in abundance his gifts---or in her misgivings, God would remove the abundance caused by her sins. "God blesses all of those who live the best they can for a righteous life. Amen," Sissy whispered in response to her later thought.

Sissy's overeating had begun when she was a young girl, but she wasn't yet ready (and probably never would be) to look back on her past and deal with those demons. Instead of the past and the core reason for her psychological need for eating her way to obesity, Sissy focused only on the present moment for why she'd eaten an entire box of swiss rolls. She hadn't heard from her younger sister Shelly in five days. If the five days had started on a Monday and ended on Friday, she'd think it odd that Shelly had allowed almost an entire week to pass without reaching out to her with a call or at least short visit. Against Sissy's objections and all of the obvious signs that warned her against making such an unholy commitment, Shelly had ignored her and the common sense that God placed between her own ears, and she went ahead and married that demon of a man, Leroy Blackman. Sissy was sure that whatever the reason Shelly had not paid a visit or phoned her, Leroy Blackman was sure to be behind it.

Monday rolled over into Friday evening, and she'd still not heard a peep from Shelly. Sissy retrieved her cordless phone and punched the numbers of Shelly's cell, which she'd memorized. Sissy didn't like making calls from her landline to a cell phone; she believed cell phones, computers, and other technology allowed humankind to unite in a way that the entire world of man became one, like it had been in the days when humankind spoke in one tongue before God, in his all-knowing wisdom, had divided humankind into languages so that they could no longer plan and scheme as a united force. The final hours of man would be as it had been in the days of Babylon: they'd believe themselves equal with God because together they'd believe there was nothing impossible for them to achieve. Fire and brimstone would rain down from the heavens and remind them of the power of the one and only true God. "Praise God almighty," Sissy whispered. Sissy somehow held the belief that her cordless, her thirty-five-inch tube television, and her Sony radio (which she used to listen to gospel music and the numerous networks geared toward religious sermons and news) weren't part of the evil in technology contributing to man's downfall.

In the presence of company that came to visit her from time to time, her thirty-five-inch screen was turned to one of the several all-gospel networks. However, when she was alone, she would flip through the channels depending on the time of day until she found one of her favorite programs. She got a kick out of *Matlock*, old reruns of *Leave It to Beaver,* and *What's Happening.* Her favorite show of all was *The Price Is Right.* She got a kick out of trying to guess the correct prices of everyday items, and she was excited when she was closer to the actual retail price than guest on the show.

Shelly's voice was reaching out from the empty space between her cell and Sissy's cordless, interrupting Sissy's private thoughts. "Hi, you've reached Shelly. I'm unavailable. Please leave a message, and I'll return your call soon as possible. Have a blessed day."

After the beep, Sissy left her message. "Shelly, haven't heard from you all week. Hope all is well." *Something ain't right, and you know it,* the voice, which she'd come to know as God's voice, whispered in her head. She kept speaking into her cordless as if she didn't have an eerie feeling that something terrible had happened to her sister. "When you get my message, give me a call. If I don't hear from you tonight, I'll see you in church in the morning." After leaving her message, Sissy disconnected her call. She'd planned on taking a shower, slip into her night gown, and drink a cup of hot tea while she read a chapter from the Bible. She was worried about her sister and that demon of a husband. Husbands didn't step out on their wives with other women. Husbands didn't spend more time in places of debauchery like strip clubs or juke houses, drinking, smoking, and lusting, than they spent with their wives. Husbands didn't abuse their wives mentally or physically on account of being miserable with the lives they'd made for themselves.

Sissy could feel the anger, her hate of men and their lustful inclinations that tainted the purity of womanly creation. "Forgive me, Lord Jesus," she said, giving a prayer to fend off the attacks of sinful thoughts and memories. "Forgive me, wash me, and make me whole.

Give me the strength to combat evil in its many forms. Thank you, Jesus. Thank you for your countless blessing. Amen."

The prayer to her holy savior calmed her nerves, enough so that she was able to take a shower and change into her night gown. She meant to go to her bedroom, lie in bed, grab her King James Bible, and sit with her back resting on three soft pillows. She didn't make her way to her bedroom and her queen-sized bed, which she'd noticed springs squeaking and complaining more each day due to her growing body. *Can I outgrow a queen-sized bed?* She wondered. *Will I have to upgrade in size to king? And what if I expand beyond the king-sized bed? What then?* The worrying about Shelly had already stirred her nervous reaction: the need to eat when she was upset or stressed. IT went past her ability to control after she'd worried about having to move from a queen bed to a king.

She walked past her bedroom, her fatigue and even her King James Bible no longer important. She needed to console her mind, and the only way she could do that was by having something filling in her stomach. She opened the refrigerator door, and her eyes moved from left to right, stopping for a minute at fried chicken parts, two thick drumsticks and a thigh. Her hand reached and then paused over a bowl of yesterday's cornbread. Then she remembered the chocolate cake. She'd eaten half of it two days ago; she'd had a bad day and had been laughed at by a group of teenagers while she sat in a corner booth far from the crowd of customers arriving at the IHOP for morning breakfast. The teens had noticed her and had laughed because of how she had to squeeze into the booth, her stomach and breasts pushing against the edge of the table. She'd ignored those truculent adolescents and had eaten her breakfast of six buttermilk pancakes covered in hot maple syrup, whipped cream, and strawberries. She'd managed to keep her dignity and not show them her pain; they'd pay for their sins when the Lord returned. That thought had allowed her to smile as she walked past them while they giggled and slapped hands over their mouths. She'd arrived home, and the encounter with the teens nagged at her so much that she couldn't enjoy *The Price Is Right* or settle enough to pray or read her Bible—not until after she'd eaten half of the chocolate cake. After that, she'd felt much better, even renewed.

She retrieved the remaining half of the chocolate cake from the fridge, removed the cake cover, set the cake on the kitchen table, and then sat down in front of it. She felt better about life and about herself even before she'd taken a fork-sized section out of the cake and placed it into her mouth.

She consumed the remaining half of cake in less than a half an hour. Now she could focus on what she'd do if Shelly didn't call tonight, and if she was a no-show for Saturday morning worship. Sissy and Shelly had been raised as Seven-day Adventists, which meant Saturday was the most important day of the week. It was the Sabbath, the only day God asked of his children to rest and abstain from all labor, because it was the day God rested from his day after all he'd created; the seventh day was holy.

For eight years, her sister had been married to that demon of a man, Leroy Blackman, living in the close proximity of his sins, of the desires Sissy couldn't bring herself to think of. Shelly had to fulfill the requirements of being the wife of that snake in human skin. Eight years in the belly of the beast, in the depths of darkness … Sissy couldn't imagine it. Shelly managed to keep true to her beliefs as a faithful Seventh-day Adventist. She hadn't missed a Saturday sermon at the Adventist Church that they'd been attending since they were young girls. Sissy hoped her sister showed up for service in the morning. If not, although Sissy despised the thought of having to do so, she would be forced to walk into the hell that was the front door of the home her sister shared with the imp of Satan.

2.

"Jesus is coming, brothers and sisters. He won't be meek. He won't be a babe in a manger. He won't be the same Jesus who laid down his life to save the world. He'll return as a lion, as a king, to claim his throne to gather in his sheep. Will you be ready, brothers and sisters?"

The Reverend Perkins stood behind the preacher's podium. He was a large man, though not obese like many of the women who made up the majority of his congregation. He'd been an athlete in his secular life before he'd discovered a more purposeful endeavor on which to focus his efforts. Rumor had it—although the Seventh-day Adventists would never admit to gossiping among one another, as other denominations were known to do—that Reverenced Isaiah Gerome Perkins had been a big-time college football player back in the nineties during his time at Mississippi Valley State. Later, he'd played professional football for the Kansas City Chiefs. He'd lived the life of a young pro athlete with more money than he'd known what do with. Like most young men who came from nothing and were propelled into a life where they could purchase an abundance of material, along with fleshy desires, Ike (as Reverend Perkins had been called before he'd been transformed by God's holy inspiration into a man more fitting of a holy man's name) had lived the life of a sinner. He'd sinned with his body, and in his mind, he'd made such a mockery of the heavenly father's word and laws.

Then God decided to bring him back down to earth, reminding him who was in charge. Ike's knee was busted while he had been trying to make a tackle. He'd been blindsided by a big lineman. Ike eventually got over his depression of not being able to have his sprit lifted by the screams of admiration from thousands of fans, who yelled so much they'd drowned out the voice of God. Reverend Perkins later realized he'd not been blindsided by the lineman; the real hit, the one he'd not seen coming, had come from God. After he'd discovered he wouldn't play football anymore, he'd believed his life had come to an end. When he began to pray and listen to the voice of God, because the ear-shattering screams from the fanatic crowds had ceased, Reverenced Perkins understood the blindside hit had been a wakeup call from God. It hadn't ended his life—it had saved it.

Sissy sat in the front row on the right side of where Reverend Perkins preached. She'd read or heard that the soldiers of God always lined up on his right side directly behind his mighty, strong arm. Of course, the reverend wasn't God, and she'd never worship a man, not even one as faithful as she believed Reverend Perkins to be. However, she did believe the pastor to be the leader of his church and the messenger for God, delivering his words of wisdom and love to his flock. She liked the idea of being on the right side of where Reverend Perkins stood and passed on to his congregation the words of the gospel, inspired words given to him by the Lord.

Sissy wasn't able to focus on Reverend Perkins's sermon. She hadn't shouted her "Amen" or "Yes, Jesus" phrases that she and the other women sitting in the front pew's sang out each Saturday, in competition with one another over whose praise was the loudest. She squirmed in the pew like a young girl who had no patience because the sermon seemed as if it would never come to a close. For an hour now, she had spent more time looking toward the front entrance of the church, hoping but losing faith in each passing minute that Shelly would arrive and make her way down the aisle, late but no worse for wear. Reverend Perkins's sermon was nearing its crescendo; his voice would rise with the intensity of his speech and urgency of his request, demanding that someone rise, and walk to the front of the church, confess, and ask for forgiveness for the sins of life. In the moment of joyful revelation, when a sinner came to know and love Jesus, Sissy could only think of her sister and what had become of her. For the first time in all the time Sissy could recall, even the eight years Shelly had been married to the Imp of Satan, her sister had not missed a Saturday church service.

3.

By midday, the sun had reached a boiling temperature, and Sissy was sure if she tested the theory, the hypothesis claiming that when the sun reached the temperature that caused water to boil, if she cracked an egg and poured the contents onto the street, it would begin to sizzle on the concrete like it was in a skillet over a stovetop. The air compressor that transformed hot air from the outside into cool air through her car's vents had gone bad four months ago. Inside the metal and fiberglass box that men placed on a set of four wheels, constructing a combustible form of energy that allowed the box to travel long distances at fast speeds, it was a death trap. The sweat falling from her forehead dripped from her head and into her face. Some of the salty water poured into her eyes and on her lips. The sweat was like rain that fell over windshields of commuters, blocking clear views of the lines that divided eastbound and westbound traffic. Her heavy sweating caused Sissy to use the sleeve of her blouse as a windshield wiper to clear water from her eyes.

Like every other living soul born in humankind's modern world—a planet of people living their lives in a hurry—time was Sissy's enemy for getting things done, because there was never enough of it to accomplish a task. Men, in their illogical way of thinking and doing things, decided rather than simply slowing life's hectic pace so that time and speed could cohabitate within the same environment, they'd arrive at irrational decisions. Instead of peace, they decided on war; instead of love, they thrived on hate; instead of slowing life to a human pace, men constructed means of transport that increased their speeds. Lives meant to travel from one place to another at slower and more natural speeds zipped from one location to another, creating more and more things to be completed in the same twenty-four-hour day that could not change.

A few sweat drops got past her cotton blouse sleeve and entered her left eye, stinging her dark brown iris. "Fudge rockets," Sissy cursed as the sweat burned her eye. "Fudge rockets. Gosh darn it. You're such a chocolate teapot. Cotton-headed, ninny-muggins." Sissy used these phrases instead of actual curse words. She blinked her left eye until the sting from the sweat lost its effect, and the only remainder of the bite from her own sweat was the bloodshot color in the whites of her eye.

Sissy felt like a cotton-headed ninny-mugger for leaving church seconds after Reverend Perkins dismissed the congregation. She'd been expected to shake hands with the members along with the other elders of the church as they moved from within the walls of God's house and returned to the devil's playground. It was not because she'd forgotten or didn't want to participate in the weekly ritual. She hadn't followed the normal, expected routines of her morning for the exact same reason she'd heard but not really listened to Reverend Perkins's morning service. The whereabouts of her sister occupied her mind so much so that she couldn't focus on routines, even those she held in high regard.

She'd left church in a hurry, walking out of the front door ahead of teenagers making a dash for it. She'd beaten the majority of the teens to the door, even squeezing past one young man who, to her, had been lollygagging like some chocolate teapot, like one of those kids she didn't have the time or crayons to explain things to. He gave her a surprised, befuddled look she'd expect from a heavy mouth breather.

The parking lot was filled with numerous vehicles, and it caused her to freeze like a deer standing in traffic. Her inability to move had been caused by the fullness of the spaces. Sissy always arrived early and left late for church service, and that hadn't allowed her to see what the lot looked like when all of the parishioners had arrived. Her four-door 1987 Thunderbird was not easy to see within the herd of motorized vehicles.

After shed found it, she drove from the church parking lot onto route nine, headed east. She'd drive through Greenwood, past Indianola and Mississippi Valley State (where Reverend Perkins had played football). She hated that a place of higher learning featuring a devil was where 99 percent of the student population was supposed to go after they'd graduated high school, in order to become the leaders of the African American community. Sissy and other members of the Seventh-day Adventist church had petitioned that the use of the school's sports team's mascot be changed to something else—if not spiritual, at least not demonic. Nothing had become of their movement because as it turned out, Sissy and her flock had been the only ones in the community to care. In the end, Sissy and her group of religious zealots, as they'd been referred to in the Indianola and university papers, withdrew their petition and left the university, its board members, and the students to continue rooting for the devil.

Her Thunderbird caused her to feel as if she was a time traveler because of the unnatural speeds it allowed her to reach. Time travel was an illusion because no matter how fast one drove, flew, or rocketed, one would never catch time because it was always seconds, minutes, hours, or days in front of or behind the person. It left one only in the present moment, the here and now. For Sissy, behind the steering wheel of her light blue Thunderbird, the backs of her thighs were wet with moisture and stuck to the tan leather seats. She was sweating like a prisoner locked into a small box under the sun as punishment. In the present, she didn't know the whereabouts or physical condition of her sister.

When she was past the college with a demon for a school mascot, she was less than twenty minutes from downtown Inverness. The drive through the town was no more than a block. It was more of a ghost town than a place where living people did business. When she drove through the dead town, she'd continue on route nine for another five or six miles, deeper into the Delta, where civilization and neighbors were separated by miles of swampland and rows of cotton fields far as the eye could see. Shelly's imp of Satan husband, the infamous Leroy Blackman, had married her sister and moved her from a modern home constructed of real building materials to one put together with leftover, unwanted parts, causing it to resemble in appearance (although not in strength) Frankenstein's monster. Sissy's hope was that Shelly would answer the knock on her door that with a good reason for not calling. Perhaps her cellular had been dropped or had fallen into a puddle of water; they were sensitive, or so Sissy had heard. Perhaps Shelly's vehicle, her black Volkswagen (which Sissy could never mange to squeeze her rear into the seats of), had stalled or had a flat tire, and that imp of Satan had refused to rise form bed because he didn't care about his wife's spiritual emotional or physical needs.

Sissy drove through the block-sized town without noticing she'd been deep in thought concerning her sister. She was closer to learning the truth of where Shelly was. And that is all which mattered.

KISS ME, KILL ME

4.

THE CLEANING HAS been difficult but thorough. Leroy had got on his hands and knees with a green scrubby, like those that Shelly used when the grime on her favorite cooking pots and pans stuck to the stainless steel. He'd mopped the kitchen floor four times, having to empty the red-stained mop bucket and wring the tainted water from the dirty mop head after each cleaning. Shelly was dead, and the knife imbedded in her chest was a sharp kitchen blade that belonged to the set Shelly used daily to chop carrots, slice tomatoes and celery sticks, or carve ham. The tip of the blade could not be seen because it, along with three or four more inches of sharp stainless steel, was inside Shelly's chest, over her heart.

Leroy mumbled to himself about his bad luck and how he wished he could turn back the hands on the clock to eight years ago. Instead of standing in the courtroom waiting for Shelly Cousins to repeat vows, knowing what he knew now, he would have reached into the pocket of his slacks, took that gold band, and thrown it as far from Shelly's finger as possible. He'd made the wrong decision eight years ago, and every day he'd been paying the price for his actions. But the penitence he'd paid over the years imprisoned to Shelly would be a vacation paradise compared to the stiff punishment he'd receive if someone discovered her body lying on the kitchen floor with a knife sticking out of her chest.

Leroy wasn't sure whether he'd killed his wife; he'd been drunk and had done some crazy shit last night, so he might have on account of her calling him a worthless alcoholic.

24

He could have come home after drinking, boiling hot from anger, the moonshine, beer, and whisky heating his temper like fire beneath a pot. Sure, he could have had enough booze and the drunken courage—or rather, foolishness—to snap and lunge at Shelly with the kitchen knife. He had decided to learn more, and later to find out where the Creole lady lived. He'd get answers from her, force her to fill the gaps in his memories.

He paused from his cleaning lowering his head so that his eyes were only a few inches from the wood floor. He studied the plywood planks as if they were chapters in a book he needed to memorize in order to pass a test. One drop of blood could be enough evidence to send him to the electric chair, where he'd fry like a carp at a family reunion fish fry. Shelly was dead, and he may or may not have killed her. He'd decided to not worry about what he didn't know—no reason to concern himself with facts he did not have a grip on. Shelly was dead, and having the handle of a kitchen knife sticking from her chest wasn't a natural way a person was found stiff and cold. Fact number two: Shelly had been killed at home while he'd been passed out drunk in their bed, with not a bump or bruise on his body. Fact number three: there wasn't anyone else to blame, and when the cops started looking for suspects, the boyfriend or husband was first on their list. The important thing was to stay calm and get rid of any evidence that may be used against him. That evidence was the blood on the kitchen floor and his wife's corpse.

Perhaps he should feel some sadness, some remorse over Shelly being dead. He'd wondered what it would be like if she got into an accident and didn't survive the impact, or if she inherited the cancer cells that had killed her mother. He'd even fantasized about wrapping his hands around Shelly's scrawny neck and choking the life from her. But he'd only imagined it; he'd never gone further than slapping her across her cheek or the back of her head.

He'd studied the kitchen floor and didn't notice anything large enough to be seen by human eyes. After he dumped Shelly's body, he'd come home and scrub the area again. He looked at the clock hanging on the entrance to the kitchen. He'd discovered Shelly sometime around seven thirty in the morning when he'd stumbled his way into the kitchen. He had been paralyzed for about an hour after discovering her body, like some prehistoric caveman trapped for thousands of years in a block of ice. Then the freeze thawed, and his body—and most important, his mind—began to function. He knew the first thing he needed to do was get rid of the evidence, because no matter whether he did it or didn't, the evidence didn't look as if it would favor him. He'd be like that doctor in that movie Harrison Ford made, where he had been thought to have killed his wife. The man hadn't, but no one believed him on account of the evidence stacked against him. There was no proof of a one-armed man.

Leroy chose not to call the cops because if they didn't believe he didn't do it, then he'd be sent away like Richard Kimble had been, and he didn't think he had the smarts or skills to stay in hiding long enough to prove his own innocence. He felt sad because he thought he should, even though he didn't have any real love for Shelly; he wouldn't miss her in that way, and neither would he miss the unenthusiastic sex that, for her, seemed to be more a necessary chore than a means to satisfy her husband. Did his lack of feelings about her death make him a monster? He'd answer that question during some other self-analyzing session. He'd cleaned the blood from the floor, and he'd give another mopping and scrub later, after finding that Creole woman and interrogating her until she told him what he wanted to know.

Church would be letting out soon—the Saturday version of holy rollers, the Seventh-day Adventist that Shelly had been raised as, as had her obese sister. Shelly's cell phone, which he found on the kitchen floor next to her unresponsive meat sack, had several missed calls, most of which had come from her whale-sized sister. Shelly's no-show for the circus, where the pastor acted as a ring leader directing the entertainment for his slack-jawed, dim-witted followers, meant Sissy would make her way over to discover what had become of her sister. She'd arrive in the Thunderbird, which leaned heavy on the driver side as the tires fought to keep the car from being tipped over due to Turbo Butt's weight unbalancing the distribution of pounds per scare inch. Leroy needed to make sure Shelly's body was nowhere to be found, with no evidence of what had happened to her in the kitchen.

He decided to take Shelly for a little ride—the last one she'd ever take, unless one counted the sinking she'd do until she reached the bottom of the Mississippi River. He collected the towels, green scrubbers, and stained mop, dumping the contents in the trunk of his Olds. He was thankful for having a spacious trunk. He took back roads, hoping not to be seen, or at least not regarded in a way that when asked about it, someone could recall his presence. He drove the short distance to his uncle's home. Uncle Richard had broken his hip when he'd fallen off his roof while trying to change shingles. After he'd cracked a hip, Uncle Richard had gone to stay with his brother, Frank, until his hip healed enough that he could walk back and forth from the bed to the bathroom without needing assistance. The Mississippi's course took the river on a path behind Uncle Richard's backyard. The closest neighbors were much more than a holler away. Dumping Shelly's body and the cleaning materials without being seen was in his favor, especially at this time on a Saturday afternoon, where even Southerners who once prided themselves in rising before the sun peaked over the eastern horizon remained in bed well past the crowing hour of roosters.

Leroy backed his Oldsmobile into his uncle's backyard, maneuvering as best he could around the sunken tree stumps that still remained after the trees had been removed. He also dodged scrap metal, worn tires, and unless parts from numerous automobiles that caused his Uncle Richard's backyard to resemble a junkyard. He steered in reverse until the ass of his Olds was a few feet from where his uncle's backyard slanted down. The path of the backyard went in a downward direction all the way to where the dirt, rocks, and foliage butted against the edge of the Mississippi River.

He counted four roosters, and another fifteen hens with chicks following the mothers, using their clawed toes to kick away earth for grubs and insects. There were numerous chicks darting in and out—far too many for him to know their exact number. He saw two of the four hunting dogs his uncle kept. They were all mutts, mixtures of unknown breeds but skilled in their ability to track and corner game such as raccoons squirrels or possums. Two dogs poked their heads from beneath the porch, where they'd ventured to keep cool during the warmer hours of the day. They gave him a curious look, recognized his Olds, and returned to the shaded crawl space beneath the house. There was a lot of activity in and near Uncle Richards's house, but none of the comings or going was of the human kind.

Leroy decided to get the dirty work done. After opening his trunk, he grabbed the bucket with the stained scrub pads, the mop head, and rags. He carried it down the slanting, uneven path leading to the river's edge, tossed a few fist-sized stones into the bucket, and swung them forward and back like he was preparing to let go with an underhand pitch in a softball game. He opened his fingers, releasing the handle of the bucket, and it sailed through the air for about fifteen feet before splashing into the currents of the Mississippi. The bucket and supplies waffled for a few seconds on the surface and then fills with the red-colored water of the Mississippi, sinking into her depths. Leroy huffed and puffed as he climbed up the path. He needed to get more endurance exercise because he shouldn't be winded from walking twenty or thirty feet uphill. He placed his hands on the bumper of his, Olds standing next to his vehicle and catching his breath. His breathing and heart rate returned to an acceptable level in about three minutes.

He took a nervous look around his surroundings once again and was relieved there was no new activity. He stared at the green bulging plastic bags, nearly twenty-five individual bags. He'd stopped counting and had kept retrieving bags from the container until he'd had enough to do the job. He'd ripped the bags so they'd be wider and longer. Then he used electrical tape, two full rolls of it, to secure the bags together. Beneath the green trash bags were used paper, old magazines, spoiled leftovers, empty cans of Pepsi, and beer bottles—trash that must be removed from the house and taken to the dumpster to be disposed of, because if one allowed it to remain, it would pile up until there was no more space for the things that were important. The dead no longer served a purpose, no more than an empty beer bottle, and more like a rotten piece of meat or pizza left in the fridge. The dead, like the trash bags that bulged with unwanted and useless items, were discarded, taken away, and buried out of sight—and most important, out of range of olfactory glands, to the junkyards where human remains decayed and rotted.

Shelly was dead, and removing her from the world of the living was no different than taking out the full bag of trash. He lifted Shelly's corpse head first from the trunk. When he'd dragged her out to the hips, he was glad Shelly didn't have the same eating disorder as her obese sister. Lifting Sissy's weight would have strained his muscles and heart past their ability, and he'd probably die of a heart attack from the effort. When Shelly's limp legs finally rolled out of the trunk, he let her body go, stepped out of the way, and allowed the downhill momentum to carry her body to the bottom. He watched as her body, wrapped in plastic bags sealed together with electric tape, plummeted toward the river's edge. The plastic ripped on a few jagged rocks, and the uneven earth caused Shelly's corpse to bounce up and down hard, but for the most part the journey was as he'd pictured it. Leroy made his way down the slanted path once again. Balancing was difficult because this time he was toting fifteen feet of braided rope, similar to the type of rope cowboys used to hang cattle rustlers. He also carried about fifty pounds of scrap metal. The pipes and sheet metal were from what he'd scavenged from around his own yard. When he reached the river's edge where Shelly's corpse lay trapped between a large boulder and the trunk of a medium oak tree, he gently placed the scavenged materials and the braided rope on the ground next to her.

Her dead foot, which was already beginning to turn a purplish bruised color, had poked through the trash bag and now lay exposed. The foot was bare; somewhere the shoe that had been on the foot had fallen off. "Damn," Leroy whispered. He'd have to find the shoe before he left and make sure it sank to the bottom of the Mississippi along with its twin. He'd retrieve the shoe later. For now, he busied himself with positioning the scavenged metal around Shelly's corpse, using the braided rope to secure the pipes and sheet metal to her body. He hoped the fifty pounds of weight and the river's undercurrents will be enough to take Shelly's body to the bottom of the Mississippi, far and deep enough that she'd not be discovered. He pushed her body into the currents, and the water caused her dead weight to be lighter, the bulging green trash bags and grey electric tape, along with fifty pounds of scrap metal, floated on the surface for nearly twenty feet downriver. Then like a submarine noticing an approaching battleship, Shelly and the scavenged metal that made her casket sank. Leroy Blackman, her husband of eight years, the man who may or may not have placed a kitchen knife in her chest, stood as the only witness of her passing from this life into the next.

Leroy climbed the path behind his uncle's house for the second time. Around this time was the moment Reverend Isaiah Gerome Perkins wiped sweat from his brow with a white face cloth as the intensity of his message, of God's holy word, went from God's voice into his head, out of his mouth, and into the ears of his congregation. Leroy hadn't offered any final words of endearment as Reverend Perkins would have, in celebration of a faithful believer passing on from this world into the heavenly kingdom of God. He didn't shed tears or mourn the loss of a loved one, as Sissy and other family members and friends of the late Shelly Blackman would have done. Leroy simply climbed from the hill in his uncle's backyard, sat behind the wheel of his Olds, had hoped he'd remembered to do everything. *Forgetting is what gets you caught.* He knew that that much. He drove away, not really giving his wife any other thought except for how he'd explain her sudden disappearance, because eventually he would have to. Much as Leroy had thought in great detail of each step he'd taken along the way of disposing of the unwanted, he did forget to retrieve the missing shoe that had bounced from Shelly's lifeless foot.

Lana Monroe, the light-skinned Creole girl, consumed his thoughts. He called Big Lou, Ruby's poor excuse for a bodyguard. Big Lou lacked skills in noticing the comings and goings of patrons and making sure they didn't enter Ruby's Juke house armed with guns or knives. But like real women he was rumored to have much in common with, Big Lou was a gossip. "Creole girl? Naw, Leroy, I don't remember no Creole girl. You crazy or blind, I say.'"

Leroy hung up on Big Lou. *He's a liar or has more sugar in his tank then I suspected. Only a full-blown queer wouldn't have noticed a looker like the Creole girl.* He decided to drive toward Morehead because after Hurricane Katrina, many Louisianans relocated to Morehead; their homes had been washed away and many relocated to small towns like Morehead Mississippi..

5.

The absence of the skin-tight pink dress, along with the three-inch heels and the painted-on face, diminished her sex appeal, but only slightly. She was dressed in her everyday lounging attire: a pair of cut-off blue jean shorts that fit snug to her ass, the scarce bit of fabric barely covering her round buttocks, exposing a fleshy pillow that was soft yet firm. Covering her torso was a white sleeveless T-shirt referred to as a wife beater. Beneath the thin cotton, her braless tits, perky as two ripe plums with nipples hard as the tips of nuclear missiles, strained to break free. Lana Monroe's morning-after visual, the way women looked after the dim lighting of the club, was replaced by the more revealing light of the sun. After the booze caused men to see the world through plastic-stained goggles, blurring details of what they were viewing, the next morning usually caused them to swear off drinking to the point they were too intoxicated to tell the difference between a woman and Frankenstein's monster.   "Hi there, Chocolate," she said with a smile. Leroy froze like a teenager, forgetting everything in sight of a beautiful woman including his name. "Didn't think I'd be seeing you again so soon, honey," she said as she sashayed from her front door and went out onto the porch. Lana Monroe's accent, a deep, rich Southern Louisianan dialect, didn't sound much different from a Mississippi girl's butchering of the English language. What she'd said had sounded more like dare. Her *that* was changed into *dat,* and *dis* replaced *this,* and so on until her broken English almost sounded like she'd been speaking in another language. Lana parked her backside on the edge of the wooden porch, extending her long, smooth legs down over the stairs leading to the concrete ground that was inches from the final step. "Saw ya comin' from yer car."

Leroy moved slowly, cautiously, like he was approaching a fawn or rabbit, and he didn't want a sudden or aggressive movement on his part to scare away the creature. He placed his hand on the rail leading up the stairs, where Lana Monroe sat on her bottom on the wooden porch, just at the edge of where the stairs began. He made his way from the curb, where'd he'd parked his Olds, and walked toward Angie's Boarding House. Angie, whose last name he couldn't recall if he'd ever known it, had been one of the growing number of Black home owners residing in the primarily black, poor neighborhoods where white men still owned the majority of the property. She'd inherited her seed money to purchase a three-story, five-bedroom residential on Spring Street in Moorhead, near Delta State Junior College, where the neighborhood was still mostly located in a good section of town. Leroy couldn't remember Angie's husband's name; Leroy didn't socialize in Moorhead often, and he knew more faces than he did names. Anyway, Angie had collected on the hundred-thousand-dollar insurance claim her husband had taken out as life insurance, in case he meet with an untimely death—which he had. He'd climbed a ladder during a shift at the fish factory he'd been working at for over twenty years; that much had been in the papers. He'd climbed and fallen and broken his neck. He slipped into a coma from which he'd never wake.

After his death, Angie, his grieving widow, had lost a husband. In return for her loss, she'd gained one hundred thousand dollars. *Not a bad trade,* Leroy had thought when he'd learned of the story. Angie rented space in her home by the room, at three hundred dollars per room. She rented four rooms in total and kept the lower-level master bedroom for herself. When at full occupancy, Angie collected twelve hundred dollars cash at the end of each month.

Leroy had been thinking about Angie's boarding house as he'd driven from his Uncle Richard's home in Inverness, during the twenty minutes it had taken him to reach Moorhead. He didn't know how Angie would take to a man she didn't know knocking on her front door and asking to speak with one of her renters, especially a girl young enough to be his daughter. He'd heard Angie had strict rules. She wouldn't stand for drug users or drunks, and she didn't allow sinning under her roof in the form of fornication. No man or woman could come calling after midnight.

When Lana Monroe poked her head from behind the screen door as he'd made his way up the sidewalk leading to the stairs and front door of Angie's place, Leroy was glad to have been able to forgo any uncomfortable greetings or confrontations with Angie. But now as he stood staring at the Creole girl, lusting after her much as he had when he'd seen her in Ruby's, he felt the same young and foolish feeling that had caused him to do something stupid, perhaps even murderous. Leroy needed a drink almost more than he needed information; his lips felt dry, and his tongue felt heavy in a way a man lost in the desert felt from days without water. He pushed back the urge of needing a drink, which nagged him like a wife fed up with her husband's constant neglect of what she considered a simple request. He'd drink later, after discovering what the Creole girl could tell him about last night. Depending on what she had to say, after he'd heard it, that information would determine how much or little he'd drink.

"I, well, I was looking for you because … I, well," Leroy stammered, trying to find the correct words.

"Chocolate, ya want to know what happened after we done left the club." It took Leroy, who was accustomed to hearing the dialects of the South, a few looks into his mental "Southern slang to English" translation book to figure out what Lana had asked him.

Lana smiled, her teeth white as freshly fallen snow. Leroy noticed one tooth next to the canine on the right side, because it was capped with gold. He also noticed that she had freckles; he supposed a combination of low club lighting and her makeup had concealed

31

it last night. Now that he was looking past her breasts, legs, ass, soft cheeks, hazel-colored doe eyes, and smile, Leroy realized Lana was even younger than he'd first thought. *Probably not even old enough to have been sitting on a bar stool drinking moonshine.* Leroy's eyes darted left and right as he leaned his weight on his back foot, just in case he had to run for it if Lana's mother—or worse, her father—came to the front door, wondering what the old pervert was doing, speaking to their under aged daughter. He cursed Big Lou. *If he'd only do his job, one of which is to check identification of every underage-looking person trying to gain entry into Ruby's.* Then Leroy would not be in danger of being accused as a pervert.

Lana, who Leroy now figured to be nearer to seventeen than twenty-one, must have caught his sudden realization of the trouble he could be in by being here and speaking with her. "Don't worry, Chocolate. I'm of age. Turned eighteen just last month. Besides, we didn't do anything that would be considered indecent," she said.

Leroy sighed and took a deep breath. He was still not sure how much information he wanted to provide before he prodded Lana in order to discover how much she already knew. He looked her up and down; it was okay because, as she'd said, she was of age. He found it hard to believe that if provided with an opportunity, he'd not bedded the young, sexy Creole.

"If we didn't do you-know-what after we left Ruby's, then what *did* we do?" he asked. He felt ashamed for seeming like a college binge drinker who couldn't remember what the booze had caused him to do. Leroy wished his behavior had been limited to fraternity house pranks, where friends of a drunken and unconscious coed painted his face with red lipstick, or placed his hand in warm water, causing his mind to release the contents of his bladder into his briefs. Leroy stood in front of Lana, waiting for her to fill him in on the events his inebriated mind wouldn't allow him to recall.

"Ya don't remember?" she asked as she cocked her head to one side in that universal display of confusion that even man's best friend used when his master did something strange or stupid.

We didn't have sex, and she doesn't look at me like she saw me kill my wife and is now afraid for her own life. That means she doesn't know anything, or she knows and for whatever reason doesn't care that I did it. Or she's the one who put the knife in Shelly's chest. If she did, then she must have done so believing I thought it was all right.

Leroy's mind had so many thoughts at once that the words inside his head sounded like a swarm of angry bees, and each thought stung at his brain until he felt the only thing he could do to make it stop was to run away from his own thoughts. But there was no sense in running, because he'd learned a long time ago that a man didn't have the speed to run away from himself. Instead of running, only to later discover he'd not outdistanced his fears, he chose to stay and hear whatever the Creole girl had to tell him.

"We drank at Ruby's, sitting at the bar," she said. Leroy nodded his head up and down. He knew this much, and he wanted to skip the parts he already recalled. "Ya shared with me yer whole life story, from birth to present day. Ya told me 'bout yer mama and great, great ma, whose chair ya sat in while ya practiced your trumpet."

Leroy's eyes bugged out of his head. He couldn't believe he'd shared such intimate memories with a woman he'd just met. Booze usually didn't cause him to feel at ease enough to share his secrets—did it? Lana continued, and he listened without interrupting.

"Ya explained to me how the only time you was happy had been when playing ya horn, and how you dreamed of playing like Miles Davis, Dizzy Glimpse, or Louis Armstrong— especially Louis Armstrong, because he'd been your favorite."

Lana Monroe's retelling of last evening's events begin to spark the dead cells in his brain, bringing to life those memories he'd thought were buried too deeply to reach the surface. "We started speaking about what you'd do to have a chance to play your horn, to play it like ya think ya would have, if only you'd keep practicing, playing hour after hour, day in and day out, until you could play like Miles, Dizzy, or Louis Armstrong"

Leroy blinked, his mind jerked like a chest being hit with electric currents in order to get the heart beating again. Suddenly the memories started again. Lana's retelling of events he'd forgotten provided his brain with enough juice for the memories to start flowing like the blood to the extremities of the body.

Lana's voice had become distant in his ears, but he still heard each of her words, silently mouthing what she said as if he were a doll sitting on her lap while she reached her hand into his back, pulling at strings beneath a hole in the back of his shirt to move his extremities and mouth so that it appeared what she was saying was coming out of his mouth. Then suddenly, the ventriloquist and her dummy spoke in unison, to the amazement both. Lana begin with the statement "Then I asked," and together they said, "*Would you sell your soul for it?*"

Leroy remembered now where he'd gone, whom he'd met with, and what he'd traded his soul for. He recalled the dream that had awakened him, and the man who hadn't really been a man. He remembered again the question he'd been asked: *Would you sell your soul for it? Well, would you, boy?*

Now he remembered his reply to that awful question in a more conscious way than he had earlier in the morning. He'd said, "Yes. Yes, I'd sell my soul for it." And this time, he was positive that he had.

6.

The taunting that manifested revealed itself in a physical way. His sense of sound was the first of the five senses to relay to his mind what the laughing was meant to represent. He'd been manipulated and prodded because he'd allowed himself to ignore the obvious dangers. Like majority of dangers that lure, the bait had come in the form of an enticing, well-disguised trap: Lana Monroe. The layers of bait that covered Lana's inner thoughts were as sharp and dangerous as a concealed fisherman's hook used to snag catfish gliding on their bellies across the river's bottom.

Leroy lunged toward Lana, meaning to strike her. His right hand was open with his palm cupped slightly so he'd be sure to lay the heavy portion of his palm against her cheek bone—a technique he'd practice and mastered over the years with numerous women he'd been forced to remind of their place. *You need to learn the number one rule,* Leroy thought as he poised his right hand high over his head, preparing to bring it down fast and hard. *You don't mess with Leroy Blackman—not ever.*

Lana screamed, and the ear-piercing wail sounded like it might wake the dead, or at least rouse the neighbors and other tenants from within Angie's boarding house. People would believe a bloody murder was about to take place. Lana's screech reminded Leroy of the warning cries monkeys shouted, alerting their family members of dangers just below the trees. Lana's perfectly timed outburst caused Leroy to pause his hand mid-strike which was as difficult to do as it was for a boxer to pull back a knockout punch at the moment the bell ended the round. Leroy couldn't managed to halt the momentum of his swing, but he was able to change its trajectory. He changed the full range of his swing, causing the punishing open palm to slap hard against his own shoulder.

Lana's taunting giggle picked up from where it had ended before her scream, at the exact moment Leroy's palm made a slapping sound with his shoulder. Her laughter sounded like a child's uncontrollable cackle when being tickled.

"Stop laughing, you crazy-ass Creole witch!" Leroy demanded, his angry words spitting from between a clenched smile that formed across his face as he attempted to look jovial. He didn't want the onlookers staring at them with confusion, unsure whether the young girl's scream had been a part of her crazy way of expressing laughter, or if she'd been in dire need of assistance. Within a few minutes of observation and not seeing anything indicating that her scream had been a cry for help, folks returned to what they'd been doing before the strange interruption.

Leroy knew Lana hadn't stopped because he'd demanded it, but because she'd wanted her laughing to lessen the impact of her scream in the minds of anyone within range. She knew she could have kept on screaming until someone—a few of the rough boys from across the street, Angie with her cell phone, or numerous neighbors—came to her aid. Leroy knew Lana would enjoy witnessing him being beaten to a pulp by the boys who liked to use their fists or feet; if the fight was too much for hand-to-hand combat, they'd be quick to grab handguns they kept at their hips or tucked in their beltlines between their bagging jeans and ashy flesh. He figured she must have believed there was no need to incite early retribution on him, because his penance for his stupidity and foolishness would come soon.

"Did ya really think ya could slap me face right here on me own porch, in front of me own neighbors?" Her words were as taunting as her laughter, and it angered Leroy even more than he'd already been. "Ya be remembering what ya did now, don't ya? Your crossroads deal, and before that, what ya done to yer wife."

The mention of his wife sent shivers down Leroy's spine. *She knows. She knows what has happened to Shelly.* The thoughts made a buzzing sound in his head, and he wanted to run. Leroy shook his head back and forth in a display of denial, because he'd remember as much as he could, or at least as much as his mind would allow him to recall. He shook his head because he didn't want to believe or hear the rest of what Lana Monroe had to say. But like rubberneckers driving past accidents, Leroy couldn't close his ears to Lana's words any more than a rubbernecker can pull his eyes away from the disaster of a scene of an accident.

"Ya gave up ya wife as sacrifice to learn how to make a deal to have all ya want in life." Lana continued to open the holes in his memories that he'd rather keep closed.

Lana realized no matter how much she told of the truth; Leroy would never believe her, not in totality. Sure, he'd believe he'd been drunk enough that he'd driven to a deserted country road, and he of course had no choice about accepting the murder of his wife. But what about the crossroads, the man in black, the deal with him to provide Leroy with everything he'd ever dreamed of since being a ten-year-old boy?

"Don't believe me? Then go on back to the crossroads. Call fer him, and he'll come because you and him got a pact now—one that only death can break. Then he'll be collecting what's owed," Lana said with a genuine expression of joy.

"You, you gonna have to show me the way. I don't know how to get to no crossroads," Leroy stammered. He felt small for having to beg, for pleading like a cockered man to a woman.

"Your horn show you da way. It linked to dat place, to da crossroads," she said. Leroy stared puzzled, so she added, "Take it with ya. Place it in the passenger's seat next to ya, and you'll see. It'll take ya right to where you need to be."

The beautiful young Creole girl stood to take her leave. She turned her back to him as if he didn't matter at all. Then she paused and turned looked over her left shoulder.

"Chocolate, don't wanna see ya no more. Understand?" she warned. Then she moved past the end of the porch to the screen door, entering too far into the home for Leroy to view her.

My trumpet will know? Leroy didn't want to venture to the dark place Lana referred to as the crossroads, but Shelly was dead, and soon he'd have to explain her absence. He figured if he understood more of the reason surrounding why she'd died in the first place, then explaining why she was gone might not be as difficult.

7.

The brain has the ability to store and recall routines performed on a consistent basis, so that even when consciously you're focused on something other than the physical or mental task you're doing, you don't realize in a cognitive way that you're performing the action. Scientists who study these human behaviors, where the mind seems to function on its memory of repetitive actions, refer to the mind's independent control as being on autopilot. Leroy's brain must have been on autopilot because he had no memory of taking roads or making the turns that had been necessary for him to arrive home. He was surprised when he steered his Olds into the dirt space, where heavy rubber tires and exhaust from his engine had turned it into a barren, brown plot of earth where nothing would grow.

The morning's events had finally taken their toll. He'd been high on adrenaline for most of the day, jacked up like a man after he'd swallowed a mixture of amphetamines and pills, a system of taking drugs called highballing. The mixture of excitement, fear, and desperation had acted like a highball, but since the morning events, only the fear and desperation remained, and the combination of the two without the excitement did little to keep the adrenaline pumping.

Leroy felt tired and years older than the fiftieth birthday he'd celebrated less than a year ago, which placed him at the middle age that began the downward count toward the end of his life. Reaching the half-century mark caused him more anxiety than all the other birthdays that were supposed to mark some important milestone. In truth, if people were honest with themselves, after twenty-one, the other so-called important milestones were nothing more than common stones that were in no way unique. Reaching fifty had caused Leroy to realize how much of his life he'd wasted, and the time he could not get back. Fifty would move him forward to the next milestone, which he would drag his feet toward because he had no desire to be the senior citizen that the elder men in his family have become. He rubbed his hand over his bald head, the palms of his hand tingling upon touching the rough stubble of hair that would not grow much past a few inches. Left unattended, the places his hair would still grow sprouted from his head until his hair billowed upward and out like the mane of a lion. The hair follicles—like his once firm muscles, twenty-twenty vision, catlike reflexes, and every physical and mental ability—had diminished in some fashion. The hair follicles were like the waning muscles in his legs that caused him to struggle while climbing a simple mound of rock and dirt behind his Uncle Richard's house. Life was like a rollercoaster: they claimed to take him up into the sky like a bird or plane and bring him back to earth again, excited and thrilled because the ride evoked all of his fears, joys, and imagination in the space of time that it took to climb, dive, and spin.

He remembered the Superman rollercoaster at Six Flags in Jackson, where he'd gone with other high school seniors after graduating. They stood in long lines in June temperatures that reached one hundred degrees without shade, just to sit their rear ends into bucket seats and be fastened in. Slowly they climbed upward, just as they had been doing all of their young lives, since first day of kindergarten, until they reached the heights of their education—senior year. They walked across the stage and received the diploma promising them a future of unending possibilities and joy. The upward climb promised to send them into the stratosphere, some distant place beyond Mom and Dad, beyond high school and homework. They didn't realize it; youth couldn't see past present desires, blinded by the time and years they believed they had to figure out what was to be done between now and the future. Graduation was the top, where youth, time, and future met. When they went over the lip of the highest point they'd ever climb in their lives, all that was left to do was what they had done on that afternoon when they rode the Superman roller coaster: hold on for dear life, scream, cry, laugh, pry, and most of all hold on with all their might. Life was a one-way ticket up and down, spinning and twisting at blinding speeds that caused them to lose your breath. The rollercoaster was all they got, the ups, downs, spins, and twists, and there wasn't anything that could duplicate the first time. In life, they didn't get to go back in line to get another thrill. In life, they got only one ride, and when it was over, that was it. *Then you're like poor old me and the majority of adults still above ground, if they'll be honest with themselves*, Leroy thought. *You spend all of your time looking and thinking about the past, praying or wishing you had some way to go back in time, or at least recapture emotions and energies of youth, bottle and drink them like soda pop, and be refreshed by the youthful fizz.*

"Leroy, I know a way you can get it all back, and then some," the voice of Lana Monroe whispered in his thoughts. *"Would you sell your soul for it?"* Another voice, the voice of the man in black whose face was still a mystery to him, added.

Since waking and discovering his wife's body cold and stiff on their kitchen floor, the shock had him acting of desperation, an animalistic reaction caused by a desire to survive, rather than any focused, higher-level thought. Later, still driven by his primal nature, he'd sniffed out Lana Monroe, following clues like a coon dog instinctively followed the scent of a raccoon or possum; he had scent of something and couldn't let loose until he found it. The adrenaline had gotten into his bloodstream and spread throughout his entire body, all the way to his gray matter. Once there, like alcohol or whatever one's drug of choice may be, it affected his ability to think in any rational, coherent way. When he'd needed to function in a beastly fashion, to act on his need to survive, the rational part of him may not have been efficient. It wasn't able to put aside emotions in order to do what needed to be done. During the drive home from Moorhead, the miles he travelled without being fully conscious of doing so, the autopilot had dissolved all remaining drops of his adrenaline. Now the rational, smart, and opportunist Leroy Blackman had returned.

Leroy leaned back in the bucket seat of his Oldsmobile, the leather seats cushioning his backside. His shoulders relaxed. The throbbing of his frontal lobe hadn't gone away, but the woodpecker stopped trying to peck a hole in his skull. He thought about his trumpet, which he'd left it lying on Shelly's side of the bed, and wondered what might happen if he picked it up, pressed his lips to the mouthpiece, took in a deep breath, and slowly released it into his horn. He wondered if, his blowing through the brass cavities and valves of his horn would bring the instrument back to life. He wondered if the notes of his horn could break down the barriers of the present and past, like the note from the horn that the children of God played, bringing down the walls of Jericho. He wondered if his horn could be that brass ticket, like the golden one kids found that gave them entrance into Willy Wonka's chocolate factory, the world where anything was possible because in Wonka's world, past, present, and future didn't matter. Delicious, wonderful chocolate fueled his factory, suspending and propelling it like a time machine to anywhere Willy wanted to be.

His trumpet could possess such amazing and life-altering ability. He'd use it to purchase a new life to climb, and to keep on climbing because when he came down, he wanted the spinning, twisting, and diving to never come to an end. Since the first time this morning—and the first time in long, uneventful, agonizing years that wore him mentally and well as physically—Leroy felt as if he may have discovered a way to feel alive, to get it all back, and perhaps even a little more. He placed his hands behind his head. He showed the despondency and loathing that was beneath the mask he wore like he was in the circus, in a show where he was not the main attraction but the guy who picked up the trash and shoveled the ankle-high crap deposited by the elephants. But perhaps he could make a change and become something other than that. The thought of being something more caused him to smile.

The knocking on the glass of his window startled him. He'd been so engrossed in his thoughts, in having the life he'd always wanted, that the knocking roused him like he'd been awakened from a delightful dream. He opened his eyes after almost leaping from behind the wheel and into the passenger side of his Olds. Then he sighed in both relief and disgust. Whatever was beyond his widow was blocked by Sissy Cousins' oversized head blocked, fat face, triple chins, and hog-sized jaws. Sissy's mouth opened and closed, and he thought if he lowered the widow or opened the door, she may try to take a bite out of him like Kujo. Sissy looked rabid and was even larger than the two-hundred-pound dog. After some careful lip reading, he could make out her words that were muffled by the engine of his Olds and his rolled-up window: "Where is my sister, Leroy?"

The same place you're one doughnut away from being, lard ass, he thought. Leroy knew eventually folks would come asking questions. He'd played with several different scenarios, trying to figure out which seemed more plausible. Sissy wouldn't believe any story he told her, but she wasn't his main problem. After not getting what she wanted, to see and speak with her sister, she'd run to cops and tell them what a heathen of man he was, adding that he'd probably done some god-awful thing to her little sister. Leroy thought of how many more pounds Sissy had than Shelly, and how the size difference separated them more than the four years in age ever could. For some reason, the thought was funny to him. He laughed.

Sissy saw lines of laughter cross his face, and she believed she was the butt of some stupid joke he was telling himself. Sissy stood straight and placed her chubby hands on the rolls that bulged from her sides. She must have yelled really loudly, because this time Leroy did hear her over the roar of his car engine. "Leroy Blackman, I demand to know where my sister is!"

Leroy reached for the door handle, and he stepped out while staring at his oversized sister-in-law. He was still not sure which story to tell about why Shelly was missing. *But it really doesn't matter, does it?* he thought.

Another voice in his head agreed, adding its own silent thought, *No, my boy, it don't matter one way or the other.*

8.

Sissy demanded in twenty different ways, and Leroy said no in just as many. As he'd expected, she hadn't believed his tale of Shelly's affair, and how he'd come home from a night of drinking at Ruby's. That much of his story had been true. He figured the best way to lie was to add some actual facts. When the cops came, at least most of what he said would be the truth. He'd tell him about the argument, about Shelly's aggressiveness, and his mature way of not returning her physical or mental insults. He'd say how he'd ended the marital disagreement by leaving the house. He say to them, using the same tone of disbelief and sorrow he'd been using when telling Sissy, that he'd come home from Ruby's drunk as a skunk. Somehow he'd managed to make his way to bed, passing out and not noticing Shelly had not been snoring on her usual side of the bed.

He'd woken with a headache and a mind full of regrets that only apologizing to his wife for his inappropriate response would cure. He'd admit she'd been correct in saying he drank too much, and he'd decided to put down the bottle that very morning. He'd hoped Shelly would be lying in bed so he could apologize, and they could have the makeup intimacies couples sometime had after a heated encounter.

But Shelly had not been there. Instead, on her pillow a hand written letter that had blended in with the white color of the pillow and sheets so much so that he'd almost not noticed it. The ink looked like tiny ants marching across her pillow; that had grabbed his attention. After he'd cleared the fog of sleep and fought the hangover—results of the drinking he wasn't proud of—he realized the writing was in Shelly's own penmanship. He struggled at first to read what she'd written because as Sissy (and anyone else who'd had to read a note or message left in Shelly's own writing) knew, she wrote as if she was afraid to use the entire space of paper. She crammed all of her written words into the smallest space she could, forcing anyone attempting to read her notes to squint and focus their eyes like they were trying to thread a needle.

"Leroy Blackman, you old disciple of Satan, let me in that house or tell me where I can find my sister, so I can know she's safe," Sissy threatened. Her words, like the excess weight of her body that placed stress on her joints, strained her lungs and heart, causing her vocal cords to sound winded.

Leroy stood in the space between his door and Sissy. He knew if Sissy was able to get a downhill head of steam like a locomotive—or in Sissy's case, more like a black rhino—her thick-boned, blubber-padded body could run him down, leaving him flat as a flapjack on someone's breakfast plate. Sissy's five-feet, two-inch frame held an advantage over him in bulk, but because she carried the excess pounds, she lacked speed and agility. He could dodge, eliminating her one advantage over him. He stood his ground.

"The deed on that there house," Leroy began, crossing his left arm over his face so that the bent arm and index finger pointed behind him in the direction of his house. "The deed says that house belongs to Mr. Leroy Blackman. Nowhere on that deed is the name Sara Cousins." He crossed both his arms over his chest.

"My sister's name is on that deed too. Everything you own, she gets half!" Sissy shouted in rebuttal to Leroy's claim of ownership of the dwelling, which was nothing more than cheap plywood hammered together with nails. It was no better constructed than a boy's tree house.

Leroy smiled and opened his arms wide, like he was Moses preparing to part the sea and lead the children of Israel from bondage. "Well, like I said, your sister ain't here. So as far as you concerned, I am the final word. You might say I'm the law."

Sissy looked past Leroy, ignoring his last comment. She looked toward the windows to see if one of the curtains parted, indicating that perhaps Shelly was home but afraid to reveal herself due to her monster of a husband guarding her exit like he was one of the devil's hounds blocking the path for sinners to escape hell. "Shelly, Shelly girl! You come on outta that house! Don't you be scared? He won't do nothing while I'm here," Sissy yelled, straining her lungs and vocal cords even more.

Leroy raised his hands over his head like he was a quarterback who'd just passed for a fifty-yard touchdown in the final moments of a Sunday night game. "Satisfied? Told you she's not here. Your sister left with her lover during the night, disrespecting the holy vows she'd taken before God and Judge Marion."

"Don't you blaspheme God's name, and don't you tell your awful lies about my sister! She a good, faithful women who only made the mistake of marrying the likes of you!" Leroy intentionally spoke ill of Shelly to get under Sissy's skin knowing she couldn't help but take the bait. She couldn't allow his words to go unchallenged.

"Well, Sissy Cousins, it don't matter what you say, or what you do or don't believe. I don't have to answer to the likes of you."

Leroy had a point. He didn't have to answer to her. Someday (and soon, she hoped) he'd have to stand before God and watch as the Lord opened his holy book, the one within which he had written the names of all sons and daughters of Adam and Eve, recording their lives so that in the end, when he opened his book filled with names, along with deeds both good and bad, he'd use humankind's own sins to judge what kind of life a person had lived. Then he'd shared with the person how much good or evil was done, judge him or her by the sins, and determine whether one would be allowed past the gates of heaven or cast into the pits of hell. Sissy was certain Leroy Blackman's page would be filled with an excess of evil deeds, and when the reading and tallying was complete, he would be cast into the fiery flames of hell's furnace.

But until God's rapture or Leroy's death, whichever came first, Sissy would need a man's help to make Leroy fess up to the abuse he had likely rained downed on her poor sister. Sissy's heart was heavy as she stood helpless against the evils of Satan while one of her own flesh and blood was in need. She could imagine her sister lying in bed, her lip busted, bruises covering her arms legs. "God going to make you pay for your sins, Leroy Blackman. Going to make you pay!" Sissy mumbled as she headed toward her Thunderbird.

"Tell him I'm standing right here, waiting," Leroy responded.

Leroy watched as Sissy's Thunderbird leaned low on the driver's side, the tires sinking into the gravel. To Leroy, it was amazing one of the four tires didn't burst like a balloon from the pressure. He watched the Thunderbird until it curved around the bend, and then he made his way to his house, free again in his thoughts and the dreams that had just begun to form before Sissy interrupted. Perhaps he'd make his way to the crossroads like the Creole girls had suggested, and he discover for himself what this mystery was all about. *Your trumpet knows the way.*

GOING ON DOWN TO THE CROSSROADS

1.

LEROY OPENED HIS bedroom door twice. Once was when he'd finally rid himself of Shelly's hefty, overbearing waste of space and oxygen older sister. He'd claimed a victory in their first round encounter. It was a fight that he knew had only just begun, and he'd have to win several more hard-fought rounds before he could raise his arms over his head in a display of ultimate domination over Sissy. He worried about Sissy's next move after she'd recovered from their verbal sparring, where words stung like left jabs and a few right uppercuts and crosses. It was a feeling-out round they'd had in order to measure one another's strengths and weakness. Leroy knew Sissy would return to her corner, where she'd get a breather, assess her mistakes, and acquire advice from those she'd be able to sway to her side. Then Sissy would lead a charge with added assistance from authorities, which would increase the magnitude of her beliefs. If he wasn't careful in protecting himself, the preponderance of claims Sissy and the cops would make against him could send him to the electric chair.

The disquieted mood was caused by the uncertainty of where Sissy's next attack could come from, and how well his defenses would hold up to her constant barrage after she'd brought additional eyes ears and mouths into the fray. The anxiety over Sissy and the cops kept him from pressing his lips against the stainless steel mouthpiece and giving it a soft kiss of mostly air, a little peck to see if it would respond, if it'd moan with pleasure—a sound that would alert him of mutual desires, and a sign to increase intensity. Leroy had held off on exploring carnal desires that provided him with similar pleasures as when he was lying atop a woman, using his johnson to make her holler and scream; her sex sounds were a mixture of noises similar to fusion jazz. Leroy hadn't gone into his bedroom to see whether he and his old companion might rekindle passions they'd shared during clumsy, immature couplings in the cotton field, when he'd been too young to know practice, no matter how much effort and time one gave it, could only take him so far. Maturity and experience over time could improve inexperienced fumbling, but some were born with gifts, and others were not and would always lack in the necessary ability to reach the heights of men blessed with natural-born talents. Leroy peeked into his bedroom to take quick glances at his trumpet, which is still on Shelly's side of the bed where he'd left it at the start of his morning.

He felt an eagerness to push aside the door, go to his bed, and rouse his trumpet from long, silent years of hibernation. Having such a desire within reach made it difficult to be patient and not be overwhelmed by excitement, so much so that he'd ignore the importance of responsibility. Leroy closed his bedroom door immediately after his first peek, and again after the second. He did his best to forget about his trumpet, at least for now. There would be plenty of time for him to reacquaint himself. He needed to mop the kitchen floor, scrape tiny cracks in the wood with a toothbrush, then disinfect the entire area in bleach, and then repeat the cleaning cycle again, just to be sure.

Cleaning took his mind off of his trumpet. Worrying erased the mountainous chore of cleaning, so much so that his mind receded once again into that autopilot state, causing familiar routines like mopping and scrubbing to be completed by the autopilot section of his mind. He'd mopped and used the soft bristle of two toothbrushes to erase as much evidence of the crime as he could, and he'd done so without realizing the time or effort that cleaning of the kitchen had taken. The morning hours that began around seven thirty were now coming to an end. He looked at the clock hanging over the entrance to the kitchen and was as surprised as he had been when he'd steered his Olds into the parking space in the front of his house without remembering the trip. "Eight hours?" he whispered, not believing so much time had come and gone. Had he really been cleaning his kitchen for nearly six hours? Was it possible he'd lost so much time without realizing?

Sissy was the current albatross adding weight to his already heavy load of problems. That weight, especially of the magnitude Sissy brought, would be difficult to carry. This time he'd not meant the play on words about Sissy's weight and the heaviness of his problems, as he usually did. Sissy has not returned with men dressed in blue uniforms flashing shiny badges and brandishing weapons, along with steel handcuffs to decorate his wrists if the answers he gave did not bring satisfaction to the questions they'd ask. Leroy knew Sissy would go to the cops after he'd provided her with a story about her sister that Sissy had known had been a lie. Sissy would tell her own story, and he could imagine her jaws flapping and her three chins shaking as she spoke with an exaggerated enthusiasm that would cause her to appear emotionally instable. *Um, okay, Miss. Okay, Ms. Cousins, we'll look into It.* Leroy could imagine cops bobbing their heads up and down while never intending to rise from the comfort of idle hours, at least not before the twenty-four to forty-eight hours an adult had to be unheard from before she could be considered missing.

After cleaning his kitchen, Leroy wrote a note as best he could in Shelly's handwriting, drawing on old grocery lists and letters. It didn't have to be exact because after writing the Dear John letter, he'd ripped the note to pieces and ignited the letter with his lighter, so that most of the paper was burned. Then he threw the fire-scarred paper into the kitchen sink and turned on the water. For whatever it was worth, he staged the scene exactly like he'd later describe it. He thought about trying to shed a few tears, but when he practiced crying in the mirror, the look on his face was more the look a man had when attempting to take a crap, not that of a man in deep sorrow and pain from losing his wife to another man, so he abandoned the idea.

Leroy believed the kitchen had been cleaned as best as anyone could have cleaned it. He felt good about his story concerning Shelly's missing status. Twenty-four to forty-eight hours was plenty of time for him to figure out what the Creole witch Lana Monroe had been speaking of when she'd said he'd gone down to the crossroads and spoken with him the man in black whose face he can't quit see, and whom he'd almost seen in his nightmare. Leroy was a Southern man born and raised in the land of Dixie, so of course he knew about the crossroads and about what deals were said to be done while standing in that no-man's zone. A crossroads was a piece of earth that didn't belong to earth or heaven, but was a little piece of hell. It was the one place where Satan could manifest in flesh and bone, and where men could call upon him like they called upon God and ask of him whatever they desired. All Mr. Happy wanted in trade was one's immortal soul.

Leroy thought he'd go down to the crossroads see whether he'd been drunk enough to make deals with the man, whether Lana Monroe's stories had simply filled his mind with delusions that had seeped into his imagination and came out on the other side in his nightmare. Lana Monroe may be pulling his leg, although he didn't think so. He needed to know for himself. *Your trumpet will know the way,* Lana Monroe had said. *Just place the horn in the passenger seat, and it'll tell you which way to go.* Leroy didn't know what Lana Monroe had meant in saying his trumpet would know the way. Was it because of the connection it had to the place?

Leroy, you've come this far. Why not go a little farther up the road? He thought to himself. Shelly's dead. I may or may not have killed her—more than likely I did. If I didn't, I guess

I'm not acting like an innocent man. Innocent men don't wipe crime scenes clean, don't take the body of the wife to the edge of the Mississippi and dump her like she's trash. Men who have souls don't lie about the virtue of their wives and then write lies as best they can in their wives' handwriting. If he didn't murder Shelly, he may as well have, because he was just as guilty as the real killer. Leroy knew if what Lana Monroe had told him was true, it didn't matter. He was sure he was on his way to hell when his life came to an end, so what did it really matter?

2.

Moonlight shined over his shoulder, glowing with the lugubrious intensity of a light bulb emitting obstructed rays from beneath the shade of a lamp. The light managed to illuminate patches of darkness, but it was not enough radiance to reach darker, deeper, and more dangerous lairs, where creatures of the night reside.

Leroy drove his Olds straight, making lefts and then rights while travelling east and then south. He began to feel like his driving without knowing where he was going had become the longest game of hot and cold that he'd ever played. He drove several miles in one direction, and the temperature inside of his Olds dropped ten degrees for every mile travelled, until he felt as if the interior of his Olds was more like the inside of a walk-in freezer where fresh meat was stored for later use. Outside, the temperature had to be no lower than seventy degrees. He removed his hands from the steering column, first his right and then his left, blowing warm air from his lungs into his hands in an attempt to warm his numb fingers. Even when he turned on his heater at full blast, the space around him still felt cold, as if he was outside on a winter's day in Chicago or New York, a place where the cold froze a man to the bone. He felt like the freezing went past his flesh, travelling all of the way to his skeletal frame; it was the kind of cold where no matter how much he attempted to warm himself, the heat would not penetrate past the flesh through the icy, thick layers of frost.

Leroy had backed out of the patch of dead earth that served as a parking space for his Olds. He'd driven in an eastwardly direction for no logical reason. He'd done so only because east seemed as good as any other direction. The icy cold that seemed to only exist within the confines of his Olds found its way inside his flesh about a mile east of his home. He'd driven a few more miles and then decided to change direction, taking an exit that would lead him toward the towns of Greenville, Vicksburg, and then all of the way to Cleveland, Mississippi. He hadn't started to feel warm again until taking another turn away from the southern route and heading back north, past Inverness and toward Yazoo City.

He'd passed the exit to Yazoo City, and as he drove farther north, away from the city, the chill returned in his bones. It had been then that he'd realized his direction had affected the temperature within his Olds. He took his right hand from the steering wheel, and allowed his fingers to caress the brass-colored aluminum surface of his trumpet. Immediately he pulled away, as if he'd touch a hot stove, because that was what the frost on his trumpet had felt like. *Your trumpet knows the way,* Lana Monroe's words whispered into his ears, and this time he thought he understood the cryptic meaning behind her mysterious phrase. He swung his Olds around, dragging the rear tires in a slow semicircle until he faced the road going in the opposite direction. He'd been getting warm near Yazoo City, so he headed back to that place. He finally believed he knew what Lana Monroe had meant when she'd said the horn would know the way.

3.

The brass became so hot that he believed he wouldn't be able to keep a grip on his trumpet. Amazingly the heat radiating from his horn didn't burn his skin like he thought it might. The heat emitting from his trumpet, some inner furnace concealed within the shallow, hollow tunnels of molded brass, was shaped into the instrument that heralded the final hour of God's reckoning or roused solders to their services. Shallow pathways where air from lungs was pushed through, vibrating within the enclosed space toward the only exit where, once released, air bellowed, producing the call made by a trumpet. The furnace within tunnels of brass where air from his lungs usually moved, let him make his trumpet speak in that voice of revival or retreat, heat from within that didn't burn. Instead, it only radiated heating the body like rays of sunlight but not scorching like flames.

Leroy drove back toward Yazoo City after realizing variations of hot or cold temperatures could be used like a compass, directing him as to which way to go in order to reach his final destination. He even had a better understanding of what was accruing, although in the back of his mind, the truth of events caused him much trepidation in his decision to seek answers at the crossroads. But as he'd told himself after discovering Shelly's lifeless body, and after deciding not to call authorities, he chose instead to take his wife's remains to the Mississippi, allowing the river to be her final resting place. Then he'd contrived a scheme filled with lies that he hoped would lead authorities in pursuit of other possible alternatives, resulting in his wife's sudden disappearance. These conjectures were far from beliefs linking her absence to him. He knew that when he'd decided to wrap Shelly's body in plastic bags and toss her into the trunk of his Olds, he'd started down a path of darkness, a lightless road as deliberate and deceitful as the trails men travel when not wanting to be seen. He guessed his journey along the darker pathways those men who lie, deceive, and murder make their way along until reaching the ends of the road, where the trail narrows until it disappears and the only remaining essence is the emptiness of darkness. The black hole was devouring souls of men, much as energies of darkness swallow all matter, including light. Once they'd gone that far—and yes, Leroy did believe his journey, his actions, were leading him toward that black hole—it was too far to turn back.

You've travelled too far to go back, haven't you? The voice in his head asked.

Yes, yes I have, Leroy responded.

The trumpet did indeed know the way, as Lana Monroe had said. He'd driven for an hour or so before understanding the meaning in the temperatures emitting from his trumpet and his body. When the horn wanted him to travel in a straight line, heat radiated in front of him. When he was to turn left, his weaker side arm along, with the entire left side of his body, felt warm, as if he'd been sitting with that side of his body facing a barn fire. When his dominant side became hot, he knew he needed to veer toward the right. If his entire body got cold, he knew he'd travelled too far in the wrong way and needed to change course. The game of hot and cold went on for about an hour after he'd taken the exit toward Yazoo City. He'd driven through the small town and past shops and subdivisions lined up one after another, identical in every aspect so that if not for the forward movement, he'd believe that he'd been travelling in circles. He'd driven on down the road, putting Yazoo City's most crowded streets behind him, traveling toward the isolated pockets of land for which the Delta was known. Where the bottoms as the swamplands not suited for human living conditions took over the delta, and where nature found a place to flourish far from the needs and desires of humankind. He'd turned left—or was it right? He couldn't remember. He wasn't sure if it had been a left or right that had led him to the place where the road no longer continued.

Leroy exited his Olds, taking with him his trumpet and a flashlight that he didn't really need because the full moon, which hunters often referred to as a hunter's moon, provided enough illumination. He'd been walking in a straight line across a path covered in thick weeds, some having grown in heights reaching an average man's shoulders. He pushed through the thick brush, some of which seemed to have a purposeful intent in preventing him from reaching the end of his journey. Vines were twisting together tightly, the network of above-ground roots allowing the vines to grow in long, overlapping patterns that gave single vines four or five times the strength of one. Together, the vines and their sharp thorns (which poked through layers of outwear, pricking the flesh like thin points of needles) made forward progress as difficult as plodding through ankle-deep snow. Leroy had plodded no more than half a mile, but his progression as made difficult by the natural barriers. It felt more like a few miles than the eight hundred yards he'd actually traversed. *Where in hell is that crossroads?* He thought more than once as he endured the burning sensations in his thighs from having to use a great deal of muscle to push through the path. He would have turned back, relenting to the entire painstaking task of walking, moving aside the brush, and being poked by the thrones. He could even stomach the idea that he may spend what was left of his life behind bars, waiting in a box-sized room for his day of execution. He would have given in, but with each forward step he took, the warmth that came from within his trumpet increased. He could feel the heat building in the palm of his hand, which gripped the brass horn. He was close very close to the place he'd seen in his dreams, and although he couldn't remember his visit to the crossroads, except in those visions behind his closed lids, as if memory of it had been wiped from his mind like some traumatic event.

Leroy could see through keyhole-sized spaces, where moonlight passed through the thick, shoulder-high foliage. He can see through to what was beyond the wall of vines, thorns, and bushes, behind the living wall that concealed the mystery of what was on the other side. He could make out the clearing, an open space, a strange occurrence—something that only happened in tales like *Alice in Wonderland,* where space and time, or shape and forms, didn't make physical or mathematical sense. Leroy lunged toward the entrance and into this other dimensional world, feeling much like Alice must have felt when she first pushed her head into the rabbit hole and squeezed through it. Vines reached out and wrapped around his wrists and ankles, as if attempting to drag him away from the entrance. Or was that just his imagination? He pulled himself free, at the same time lunging forward and stumbling past the final barrier of vines and weeds.

Nothing living grew or crossed over the path. That had been the first odd thing he'd noticed. That was, if one chose to ignore the fact that a cleared patch of land in the middle of nowhere, leading from and to no particular place, was here—wherever here was. If one chose to discount that little piece of strangeness, then the fact that the road was absent of life could be said to be the first odd thing he noticed. Leroy also realized his trumpet had returned to a more normal temperature. He was here at the crossroads, where he'd conducted in a bit of trading. He needed to know the details because he'd been too drunk when the deal had been completed to recall exactly what he'd gained and lost.

He could see farther up the path, which was a mixture of pebble-sized rocks and red clay earth. He could see where the path ended, and where it met with two other paths, one veering east and the other west. Both of those paths cut short at a fence of vines and weeds. "Hey!" Leroy shouted, his voice louder than he'd meant. "Hey, anybody out here?" he asked in a more respectful tone, one he'd use if he was knocking on a stranger's door and expected an answer.

"Hey there, friend."

Leroy jumped, startled by the voice. He'd not really expected an answer to his greeting. He looked up the path no more than twenty or thirty feet from where he stood, where he could have sworn he'd just been looking and hadn't seen anyone. Now, there stood a man dressed in black, from the fedora he wore on his head to the long trench coat that looked old and tattered but didn't have a bit of road dust on it. Leroy could see the fringes of his black Victorian style shirt, a fancy man's shirt that had long gone out of style, a puffy shirt that looked like a peacock's display of feathers. The man wore of pair of black slacks along with shiny coal cowboy boots, into which the cuffs of his pants were stuffed.

"When I say friend, I don't mean it in the way most people do. Oh, no. When I refer to someone as friend, I mean it exactly for what the word entitles. Leroy, you don't mind if I address you informally, do you? I'd say we are friends, Leroy."

Leroy thought the way the man in black had stated his question, he'd told him more than asked. But he didn't offer any objections to the man in black referring to him by his first name, as if they'd been introduced years ago and now, after an extended time apart, were reuniting like old chums at a thirty-year high school reunion.

"You … you know me?" Leroy asked, hoping the man was studying him in that way a person did when inspecting details missed during first glances, when a similar shape or form reminded one of a familiar person or object. Then upon closer observation, one would realize who it was only similar in likeness, enough to spark memory but not identical.

"Sure, I know you, Leroy. I have what they call total recall. Don't forget a place, name, or person. Got 'em all stored up in here," he said, raising his arm and pointing a long, skeletal finger toward his head.

The pliable layer of skin between Leroy's eyes wrinkled as he squeezed his brows together to focus his sight. Leroy couldn't see enough of the man's face beneath the rim of that fedora, which cast a shadow over details of his features. Leroy believed he could have been so drunk that he'd not recalled being led to this place; often more times than he'd like to admit, he had awakened after a night of binging in an odd place, or having lost hours of time with no recollection of how'd he gotten to the place or where the time had gone. But he didn't believe that he'd forget meeting the man in black, if he *was* a man. Leroy believed that beneath the tattered black coat and the rim of the fedora, there resided something other than the flesh and bone of human identity,

"Can't say I see my customers so soon after a purchase. Not saying you're not welcome, just that I'm surprised. And Leroy, I'm not often surprised. Neither can I say I much enjoy the unexpected turn of events."

Leroy felt as if the man in black was speaking to him in a tone similar to a teacher's impatient and disapproving modulation used when addressing a student who had shown up to class without his homework. The voice said, "Go on, now. Tell me the whopper of a story that will be the excuse for not having completed your assignment." The inflection was the same vocalization used by a mother daring a child to continue with the lie.

"I, I, I ..." Leroy's words came out in a stutter, as if sight of the man in black had damaged that section of his brain that controlled speech

"Leroy, I don't do refunds. This isn't Wal-Mart, where you get to purchase a service or item and then decide you no longer desire it. All transaction are final." The man's voice doesn't sound like an old high school friend, or even a charming salesman greeting a former customer. Instead of a friendly gent, the inflection in his voice had the tone of an ass kicker, a man who had placed his black cowboy boot to many backsides. Leroy's eyes veered toward the ground, taking an eyeball guess on what size those ass kickers may be. *They've gotta be at least a size twelve,* he estimated. He was sure many men had those size 12s imprinted on their backsides for having traded in words with the man in black. Leroy had no intention of mixing it up with whatever or whomever this fella was; he'd rather take that swing at Big Lou. Win or lose, in that fight he'd come out better from it than trading verbal or physical blows with this fella.

"No, no. I'm not returning nothing. I, I ..." Leroy pinched his index finger, hoping the pain would distract his nervousness and end his stuttering so he could complete a sentence without sounding like Elmer Fudd when the antics of Bugs Bunny befuddled him. "I was here last night." He states rather than ask, because with the man in black acknowledging him in a personal way, he was sure they'd already met. If that bit of information was true, then the fact that he'd come here last night was true as well. The man in black leaned against a dead tree trunk that in its death had fossilized, becoming hard as stone. Leroy felt like at any moment, the man in black would laugh at him and say in the sarcastic, taunting voice of Bugs, "*What's up, doc?*" Right before he dropped an anvil on Leroy's head.

Leroy cleared his throat and began again, this time speaking slowly, focusing on each syllable in order not to stutter the words. "I don't remember coming here, or speaking with you. Don't remember much about the other night at all. I woke up ..." Leroy was almost going to leave out the part about discovering his dead wife, but he figured that was something the man in black was already aware of, so he told the story just the way it happened.

"Well, well, Leroy. That is a mighty fascinating tale." The man in black didn't seem at all shocked by Leroy's story—not even the part where he'd admitted to discovering Shelly's body, wrapping it in plastic, and dumping her corpse into the Mississippi. He didn't ask Leroy one question about how he felt about his wife's murder, or if he'd been the one to do it; he didn't seem concerned at all about Sissy or the cops who were sure to pay Leroy a visit sooner or later. The man in black's only concern was that Leroy hadn't played his trumpet. He pointed his long, skeleton index finger toward the hand in which Leroy was holding his instrument. "Why haven't you played it? What's the holdup, man?"

Didn't you hear me? I said I found my wife's dead body, that I may or may not have murdered her, that I was too drunk to remember coming to the crossroads, where apparently I've sold my soul to a demon. Haven't you been listening? What about Sissy, the cops, the electric chair? Doesn't any of this concern you at all? Because it sure as hell scares the life out of me. Leroy thought of this in the blink of an eye, but his only response to the man in black had been in reply to the question. "No, no I haven't," he said.

The man in black unfolded his arms and moved away from the dead bark of the tree. He moved slowly and menacingly like a predator toward where Leroy stood. Leroy could see the details of his face, a visage only inches away from his own. Leroy had to lift his head in order to look into the eyes of the man in black. A dark blackness filled the spaces where blue, brown, hazel, or green orbs should be floating in milky white sockets. Under the brim of the fedora, it was like beneath stones concealing the entrance of lairs of deadly serpents; like behind steel bars constructed to cage dangerous beasts and men alike; like the blanket of night that covered the world, blinding eyes to evil that transpired within the darkness. The dangers and evil intent, more than the physical shape and form that identified a man or beast, was present beneath the fedora. The utter foolishness of anyone daring or ignorant enough to lift, enter, or uncover, the abodes of creatures whose only promise was certain and painful death—this was the face Leroy saw, the face of the man in black.

Physically, if taking only a passing interest or viewing, with dull thinking minds incapable of identifying a deadly predator from a harmless, nonthreatening life-form, one would not see past the regular-looking fella, the one with the dark eyes and dark flesh. The man in black could be anyone's brother, son, or husband; he looked like any John, Jim, or Joe one would see at the market, on the street, or in a tavern having a couple of drinks before the Sunday night game. He had a regular man's face, nothing causing one to think more or less of him in looking. One minute his face may remind someone of an uncle, the next of a brother or cousin. He simply looked like everyone a man had ever known and seen, or simply like no one familiar. One minute he reminded Leroy of Miles Davis, dark in complexion and mood, the countenance of man in constant conflict with himself, sullen and complex at the same time. Then if he turned his head, another angle made the man in black look like he may resemble Dizzy instead of Miles, hard and soft faced at the same time, a man troubled but not allowing himself to carry burdens to his grave. If Leroy took another glimpse, the man in black may look like Louis Armstrong: regal, proud, playful, and joyous.

But Leroy was able to look past the many faces. He thought he could because the man in black desired it, wanted him to see his true face to see the hidden dangers beneath the fedora, to know that he, evil, had an identity. The man in black revealed beneath his black fedora desire, rage, lust, envy, deceit, and betrayal. Standing before him, regardless of what face he wore, those images didn't mean a damn. Even if he'd taken another form, one familiar to those who believed in such places as heaven and hell; if the man in black had shed his human face and taken the shape of man's idea of what evil looks liked; if he'd sprouted horns from his head and a tail from his ass—even this image paled in reality to what this beast truly was. He was that great white whale that men chased the beast that had scarred and crippled humankind, leaving a darkness within him that could not be sated by light or truth. It was the beast man must forever hunt, no matter the cost of flesh and bone or spirit. Man would traverse the endless seas, reaching into the depths of the sea and their own darkness to cleanse themselves, to make right the great wrongs of their lives.

Leroy stared into the depths of the true face of the man in black, past the raised cheekbones, the narrow and somewhat sunken face of Miles, the swollen cheeks and round face of Dizzy's, the wise eyes and knowing smile of Louis Armstrong. He looked deep past the physical identifiers that had an ability to conceal. He stared like Ishmael had when looking upon Captain Ahab: enlightened for a moment, having an ability to see beyond what crippled a man physically to the truth of who and what he had become. But before he could see the forces that drove a man to be what Ahab had become, what he himself had become, he looked away and lowered his chin to his chest, his eyes focusing on his feet and the rocks and dirt beneath them.

"Play it. Put that mouthpiece to your lips, and play it," the man in black demanded.

Leroy lifted his trumpet in trembling hands. He could not tell whether they were trembling from nervousness, excitement, or fear. When the steel mouthpiece touched his, lips he didn't think; he simply responded to the old feeling, the one that felt like kissing a former lover after years apart. The natural feeling of knowing what to do and how to do it without having to think, the autopilot response—except that he was aware of what he was doing, alert to every detail, his senses grown tenth to the power of whatever current number they were. Fingers glided across three valves without having to think which one to touch to produce a note. He'd breathed life into his horn, and now the instrument was giving back the force in double of that he'd given it, that living again force that renewed a man and washed him clean of all his ills and despondencies, the constant regrets of not having done something more with life, of not having risked to gain a greater self-worth. The trumpet he'd forsaken, the friend he'd known since his young life, a companion he'd believed that would propel him from the cotton fields, small towns, and small dreams of those around him. The notes came one after another, forming a melody of music that sounded like a combination of jazz and blues, life and death. *This is it, man. This here is all I need,* Leroy thought.

The man in black raised his hands and began clapping them, his skeleton-thin fingers sounding like twigs being snapped apart each time they came together. "Leroy, my friend that was mighty good. You haven't lost a thing. In fact, I'd say you've gotten even better."

Leroy couldn't understand it. He'd not played in over twenty years. The man in black was right. Leroy believed his ability with in playing the trumpet has improved.

"Now, you take your horn, play it much as you desire. We're gonna go places, you and I, Leroy. We're going to travel to places where we can play for money, fame, women, and whatever the hell else we want."

Leroy smiled, nodding his head in agreement with what the man in black had to say about his future. But he couldn't help worry about a few things that may interfere with his future plans. What if someone discovered Shelly's body? What if Sissy got cops to investigate deeper into Shelly's disappearance? What if he went to prison? What if a judge sentenced him to lethal injection or to the electric chair? There were so many what-ifs that could interfere with his glorious future plans.

"What if it all comes crumbling down?" Leroy asked, hoping the man in black had some miraculous plan to get him out of this jam.

"Don't you worry none about Lana Monroe. She is on our side and what's good for her, is what is best for us. If you have any trouble with Sissy Cousins or the cops, you just call me. Don't do or say anything stupid. You just give me a call, and we'll work it all out together."

Leroy felt good that the man in black seemed to be on his side. If anyone could help him out of this jam, it was the man in black. He'd trust in his wisdom and not be afraid or worried about his obstacles. Leroy turned to leave the crossroads and then stopped to look back at the man in black. "How I am going to contact you when I need you?" he asked.

"Just give me a call."

Leroy nodded but was still confused. "But I don't know your number."

The man in black laughed. "Just pick up your phone and ask for me, and I'll answer."

Leroy nodded again, still unsure, but he didn't want to question the man in black on everything. However, he had one final question, and he didn't believe the man in black would mind if he asked. "When I call for you, whom should I ask for?"

The man in black placed his long fingers to a chin that shifted from Miles's long, narrow chin to Dizzy's thick, round cliff, to Louie Armstrong's square, manly jawline. "Just ask for Moody Johnson."

PART TWO

INTO THE DARKNESS

"I'm not me anymore."

"I am the emptiness you feel at 2:00 a.m., the tears with no meaning, the pain when you smile. And I didn't come alone—I bring my closest friends. We are the scars that cover your body, the voice you despise but soon learn to trust. I am the only thing you will feel."

"Deep inside, where nothing is fine, I've lost my mind."

THEY COME KNOCKING

1.

T HE PART OF the calling where he was to be a consoler, providing peace of mind to God's children during their difficult times on earth, filling in as he could, knowing whatever words of comfort or enlightenment he could offer would pale in comparison to God's holy word. When members of his congregation came to him in order to have answers to questions causing them to struggle in body, mind, and spirit, he was supposed to provide them understanding, comfort, and most of all a reason for why God had seemed to fail them in their hour of need. The mountainous endeavor was overwhelming, the responsibility of being a shepherd to sheep that were not his own, entrusted to his care until the real leader of men returned to claim his flock. The spiritual wanting was immense, so much in abundance. He was often fearful. A small church in a small town with a preacher whose faith waned from time to time because, like members of his congregation, he too often wondered why God allowed so much pain and suffering to take place in the lives of those he claimed to love.

The Reverend Isaiah Gerome Perkins stared at the black Bible, the King James Version, engraved with the words Holy Bible in big, bold, gold font. He closed his eyes, waiting, hoping that God would inspire him with the correct verses to read so that he could enlighten and comfort not only the spirits of his congregation but also his own restlessness.

"Excuse me, Reverend Perkins." The voice of Linda, a thin, mousy-voiced women with a stereotypical librarian persona, came through the arm-sized crack in the door she'd made when she reluctantly opened it. Her grey eyes behind the lenses of silver reading glasses veered toward the brown plush carpet instead of upward and across the room where Reverend Perkins sat behind his desk. "I knocked, but you didn't answer," she said, apologizing for her interruption.

Reverend Perkins waved his hand in a way that showed Linda she had no reason to apologize. "I was just in that zone. I guess," Reverend Perkins said, which only causes Linda to feel more guilt for having disturbed him. Linda believed that holy men, more than most, needed time to speak with God, to commune with him in prayer for all those within his congregation, and for those lost souls around the world. Only prayer of the righteous could lift them form the pits of despair and hell's fires. "How can I help you, Linda?" Reverend Perkins used a tone Linda could tell was genuine, not in an the polite way someone in customer service may ask the same question, hoping that she'd decline rather than accept the offer of assistance.

"Sister Cousins has ask to speak with you," Linda whispered, turning her head to look over her shoulder and making sure her words did not travel from the tiny space between Reverend Perkins's office and the waiting room. "I explained to her that this is not your normal counseling hours, and that it would be better if she made an appointment." Linda paused again, this time to see whether she could read the reverend's face in order to see in his expression those true feelings that visages reveal before words are spoken. "I explained to her but, she insisted. She said it couldn't wait, that it is an emergency."

The calling, God's Holy Spirit that inspired men to be messengers of his word, temporary leaders of his flock guiding them the best they could according to the inspiration God provided, required men of God to set aside personal vises and their own physical and emotional needs for the good of those in need. "Tell Sister Cousins I'll see her," Reverend Perkins said, although he wanted more than anything to spend this afternoon in meditation to deal with his own personal struggles.

2.

The four wooden legs of the chair visitors sat in squeaked from the strain of having at least three hundred pounds of flesh and bone resting atop of them. The chair was positioned on the other side of Reverend Perkins's office desk. Reverend Perkins tried to ignore the cracking wood sound as he listened to Sister Cousins, but the heavy breathing between each of her words, like the squeaking sounds made by the chair, seemed to be strained by the excess weight. The combination of both sounds was difficult to tune out. Reverend Perkins didn't look at Sissy Cousins in disgust; neither did he share with others negative judgments concerning her excess weight. Obesity was a sin, a roadblock placed in front of men and women like any other vice placed in their path, such as lust, greed, and envy. Humankind struggled with then and must ask for forgiveness for them in prayer, so that God may take the sin away. Reverend Perkins would never look at someone's sin and judge, poke fun at, or view in a vile manner, thinking himself better. *All men have sinned, and all will be judged by God,* he thought.

"Sheriff says how I don't know whether Shelly ain't run off with another man. I say I know, because even though my sister married a devil of a man, she is a good, God-fearing woman. She wouldn't be no adulterer, even though being married to that devil would tempt any woman to escape in any way she can. Shelly wouldn't, because she believes in God's word." Reverend Perkins focused on Sissy's words—not the squeaking of the wooden chair legs, not her labored breathing, not the obesity that, when allowed to gain too much of a foothold, would consume the life of host. Sissy Cousins was feeding her sin much in the same way a person lusting of flesh fed his sickness of carnal pleasures: until her consumption would physically destroy her. He would have to eventually confront her on the subject before it was too late and the sin of obesity destroyed her. But not today. Today he would provide her comfort and enlightenment, if he could, concerning her problem with her sister.

"Sister Cousins, you say it's been a week since you've spoken with or seen your sister." Sissy nodded her head, her jaws shaking for a few seconds after she stopped moving. Reverend Perkins didn't know Shelly's husband, Leroy Blackman, outside of the gossip he'd heard from whispered conversations between women in his congregation. Mostly those whispers concerned their disapproval in Shelly Cousins being married to a man not of the faith. The truth was Leroy Blackman wasn't much different from the majority of men and women who chose to serve other vices over the Lord, giving in to sins and earthly pleasures because deep down they were in pain, hurting because of some terrible, empty feeling that they attempted to replace with drugs, sex, or alcohol instead of getting on their hands and knees and praying to God for healing and purpose. He didn't know Leroy Blackman personally, but he believed he knows him on the level of personal struggles, those mountains all men climbed and fell from time to time in their attempts to reach the summit. He did not know Leroy's personal battles or how far he had fallen, but he did know Shelly Blackman. He had known her before she became Leroy's wife, and in the years during Shelly's marriage to the man Sissy Cousins referred to as the devil. Unlike the sheriff, Reverend Perkins didn't believe Shelly Blackman would have abandoned her husband for another man. Sissy Cousins was right about her sister. Shelly wouldn't be lured by the sin of adultery.

"I'll drop by your sister's house, see if I can speak to her. If she's not home, I'll talk with her husband in order to see if I can get to the bottom of this."

Sissy's mouth opened, but before she could utter a word, Reverend Perkins raised his large paw, cutting her silent. There weren't many people still catching breath who could silence Sissy Cousins or move her strong will once she'd decided on staying or going. Grandma Rose had taken care of her and Shelly when their mama had passed on to her glory, when Sissy had been eleven and Shelly was eight. Grandma Rose's heart had been filled with love, and she had the sort of heavy hands so that it took one good smack on the bottom to purge the devil from a young child's thoughts. Sissy's tongue would also stop wagging whenever Uncle Joe's eyes peeked over the top of the daily paper, making that no-nonsense face that brought his hairy gray brows together so they looked like a giant albino caterpillar. The expression frightened Sissy and Shelly, and they'd stop doing whatever misbehaving action had caused Uncle Joe to take his eyes from the paper in order to discipline them with his bug face.

When the elders of her family had been freed of their earthly bondage, released into eternal glory in the kingdom of God, aside from Reverend Perkins, only two people remained in Shelly's life who had the power to calm her temper or get her to uproot her feet once she'd planted them firmly in some belief. Shelly, her younger and more even-tempered sister, had a way of making her understand that she didn't have to attack every problem head-on, so that all of her disagreements caused her relationships to end up shattered like china after a bull made its way through the shop.

The other living person who could silent Sissy, and whose name and memory filled her with pain, anger, and regret, was Antoine Bowman. If her obsession with food, the negative relationship that she knew would eventually destroy her, had had a face and name—the features in the mind of Sissy that belong to the devil incarnate—it would look like Antoine Bowman. That frightened her more than the name of Lucifer, and she used food as a drug to wipe her mind free of him. Antoine Bowman was a depraved and evil man, an unrepentant thief who stole the virtue of s young girl's possession. No matter the penitence of physical or monetary judgments, the consequences of his thievery, like the sin of murder, could never be mended. When the thief revealed himself from the dark shadows of her memories, Sissy could not move forward or speak, not until her belly was stuffed and she was intoxicated from the gluttony, so much so that she couldn't think past the fullness of her stomach.

"I'll go alone, Sister Cousins," Reverend Perkins said. He was able to reach beyond the wall of pain that Sissy had constructed in order to guard herself, the barrier that divided her from a world filled with dangerous predators seeking to feed on the flesh and spirits of young girls. The Reverend Perkins provided Sissy with another of her comforts, allowing her to push back the bad memories just as much as her consumption of food eased her pain. The reverend provided Sissy with faith, and enough belief could move mountains, allow blind men to see, heal the sick, and cast out demons. She would not argue against the wisdom of a man of faith any more than she would have protested against her Grandma Rose's heavy hand or Uncle Joe's caterpillar eyebrows.

"Okay, Reverend Perkins. I'll wait for your call. Thank you for your time and help," she said, wrapping her meaty fingers around his hands, which surprisingly made her swollen digits appear small.

3.

Leroy wasn't sure which he'd heard first: his bedroom door open, or the voice that spoke to him. Whichever sound reached his ears and caused him to whip around so quickly he thought he might have given himself a case of whiplash didn't matter at this point. In his right hand, he held his trumpet in front of his face, to use as a weapon or as a shield to protect him from attack. His left arm was extended in front of him, and his fingers were balled up into a fist that would either deliver a hook or cross. The fist relaxed after he realized he wasn't in danger of physical harm. He placed his hand on the left side of his neck, the side that had been whiplashed, and massaged the strained muscles.

"You crazy or something? Entering a man's home without knocking? Sneaking up on him while he's in the privacy of his own space?" Leroy said angrily. He could hear the relief in his own voice because he'd been afraid the intruder would be a cop.

"Now, Chocolate, ya gonna treat me like a stranger? Thought you'd be pleased to see me." Lana Monroe stood a few inches from the entrance to his bedroom. Sunlight poured into his resting chamber through the now open door. Yellow rays of sunlight illuminated the area behind her, causing her honey blonde skin to glow like bars of gold. It was the type of radiating illumination that, once it caught a man's eye, produced a sparkle in his dull orbs. It was ignited into a flame by desires, cravings that were parasitical. The more one fed it, the larger it grew. It expanded until the host was weighed by the bulk he now had to carry.

"I thought you said you didn't want to see me no more," Leroy said, regaining his composure after having seen Lana Monroe.

"Ya sure playing that horn of yours like you was born to play it. I heard you all the way down the road," Lana said, ignoring his question.

Likely because it isn't important to her, Leroy thought. He'd let it rest for now, because she'd commented in a positive way about his trumpet playing. "I've been practicing through the night," Leroy proudly stated, his smile similar to the watermelon grin on the mug of Big Lou.

Lana smiled, and her pearly whites were admission enough to get past Leroy's defenses and the threshold of space separating his bedroom from the living room. "There ain't nothing like the mouth of a musician, tender and soft lips, the sort of kissers that can make sweet music emit from mouths of instruments and women alike," Lana said in a seductive, teasing tone.

Leroy could feel his johnson snaking upward toward his stomach. Lana had better be careful with her flirtations, because the serpent concealed beneath the thin fabric of his boxers hadn't fed in weeks, and everybody knew one didn't play with a worm unless one meant for it to strike. Leroy suddenly realized, because of his johnson beginning to point north, that he was dressed in his lounging-around attire: a pair of boxers and a white Fruit of the Looms T-shirt. He scanned the bedroom and finally eyed what he'd been searching for. He walked across the room, and though it was only a few feet, it felt like he was making the trip through quicksand. He retrieved his trousers and turned his back toward Lana as he climbed into his slacks, right leg first and then the left. His johnson was at full attention, rigid and stiff like a solider standing in his barracks being inspected by a surly drill sergeant. He allowed his T-shirt to fall over his beltline, concealing the bulge in his crotch. He turned around in order to continue his interaction with Lana Monroe, noticing she had made herself comfortable, plopping her perfectly shaped rear on the edge of his bed. Lana's firm, young buttocks rested atop sheets, a mattress, and a box spring that his wife had laid her body upon. Leroy wondered if Lana Monroe realized she was sitting atop the bed of a dead woman, or if she did know, whether she'd cared.

Leroy still wasn't sure if Lana Monroe was the one who'd killed Shelly, or if she knew who did. Perhaps she'd come because she knew he'd done it, and now she was here for some kind of shakedown. She'd be in for a huge disappointment because he didn't have anything worth the time or effort it took for a blackmail scheme.

"I've been thinking, Chocolate" Lana Monroe began before Leroy's mind could conjure more fantasies concerning the reason for her unexpected visit. "Thinking that with yer new slate on life, ya need a person to manage yer business." Lana leaned back on his bed, laying on the side of the bed where Shelly had slept for the past eight years. "I mean, since you're single and all now, figure you'd be needing someone to take care of things."

Leroy smiled—not a friendly smile, but a grin that said, "Oh, yeah. I see now. You got me." It was the nervous grin that precluded crazy laughter and that said, "Yes, I've gone completely insane. Lock me up in a padded room and throw away the key." *Lana Monroe isn't blackmailing me for what I have. She's blackmailing me for what she thinks I'm going to have, and just to make sure I stay on the straight and narrow, she's offering her managerial skills,* Leroy thought to himself.

"Did you kill Shelly? Did you kill my wife?" Leroy hadn't known he was going to ask the question. It wasn't something he'd planned; the thought came to him, and the words simply exited his mouth. "Did you kill Shelly? No more games. I want to know."

Lana rested her head on Shelly's pillow, folded her arms across her breasts, blinked her lashes over her hazel eyes, and studied Leroy for what seemed like several minutes. Then in a voice that reminded him of the tone that the man in black who called himself Moody Johnson had used, Lana told him what he'd started off this morning trying to learn. "We killed her, Chocolate—the both of us did it together. She was the sacrifice, the price to pay for what the man in black done give to ya. Thought ya already figured that much out for yerself."

The air didn't just go out of his lungs—it left the entire room, pushed out by the weight of the information he had just learned. It was something he felt all along might be true, that he had killed Shelly, but all the while he'd hoped that somehow there would have been someone else, if not Lana Monroe then another lunatic murderer. Anyone besides himself.

4.

Lana Monroe went about making plans for his future as if the murder of his wife, the selling of his soul, Sissy Cousins, and the cops (once they decided to do more than write traffic tickets or harass kids parked in private fields who only wanted to explore natural curiosities) didn't matter. When the cops finally got around to doing some real police work, when tickets and harassing kids gave way to a real crime, that was when they'd ask: Did that that Shelly Blackman ever turn up? Did she contact her sister? When they asked one question, they'd ask another and another, until questions caused them to stumble onto answers that led to more questions. When the questions piled up and answers didn't, that was when cops started feeling suspicious. Then like some hound having caught the scent of a piece of fatty steak thrown out in the trash, the cops, like the hounds, would rummage through whatever mess was in front of them to get to the thing they'd got scent of.

"I think we should skip the small town's altogether and go straight to Jackson. I bet Porter Walker is still managing the Steam House."

Leroy snapped out of the trance of his private thoughts at the mention of his old friend's name. He was sure he'd not mentioned Porter Walker or the blues club he operated in Jackson. He was sure he hadn't mentioned those names to Lana Monroe, not even in his drunken condition, because neither Porter Walker nor the Steam Room had been names he's spoken of in nearly twenty-five years. He was about to confront Lana Monroe to discover just how much about his personal life she knew, and how she'd come across so much information about his past associates. If she attempted to lie to him, he may slap her across the jaw with the back of his hand.

But as soon as he was about to begin asking her a few questions, there was a knock on his door, he looked between his front door and Lana Monroe, his head moving back and forth like some invisible hand was slapping him on one side of the face and then the other.

"Don't look at me, Chocolate. I don't have no guest comin' to see me at yer place," Lana said, and she raised her hands in the air, palms open.

Leroy tiptoed to the front door, but he may as well have stomped across the room; the old beams of his floor moaned and squeaked like breaks in need of new pads. Anyone outside on the porch could hear him moving about, and there wasn't any use in pretending he wasn't home. "Who is it?" he asked.

He could hear someone clear their throat on the other side of the door, "Reverenced Perkins. I was wondering if I can have a word with Shelly or with you, Mr. Blackman."

Leroy turned so he could view Lana, who was lying on his wife's side of their marriage bed. Anyone noticing Lana lying comfortably on his bed would begin to draw his own conclusions about what sort of husband and man Leroy Blackman was. Then upon discovering his wife of eight years was missing, with the only evidence of her disappearance being the word of her adulterous husband, no rational person would believe the tale he'd concocted where he, and not Shelly, was the victim. He thought about simply ordering the reverend to march back down the steps, return to his vehicle, and drive it all the way to kingdom come. But he needed to be smart and think like a victim, a spineless man who'd thought so much of his women and so little of himself that upon her leaving him for another man, he was overcome with sadness. The victim wouldn't be mad—he'd be sad, sullen, and desperate. That sort of man wouldn't order the Reverend Isaiah Perkins to get away from his front door.

"Just a minute, Reverend," he said in a tone that he hoped conveyed the emotions of a beaten-down and hopeless man. He made his way toward his bed room and closed the door. He hoped Lana would be quiet as a mouse and understood the importance of being careful and silent.

Leroy opened his front door and took the outstretched right hand of the reverend. Then he offered him a seat. Leroy begins to tell Reverend Perkins the same story he'd told Sissy. He told Reverend Perkins about the note he'd discovered on Shelly's pillow, written in her small, ant-sized penmanship. The reverend sat still and quiet, staring at him like a man who, after hearing a story that was supposed to be humorous, was waiting for the punch line of the joke so he could sneer or laugh and not just sit there with a bewildered expression on his face. *He don't believe me*, Leroy thought as he stared into the eyes of Reverend Perkins.

The fact that Perkins didn't believe his story about Shelly bothered him more than when Sissy hadn't.

"I've known Shelly and Sissy for a very long time, Mr. Blackman. Those two are as close as any two people I know, sisters or otherwise. That Shelly would run off with another man is surprising to hear in itself, but for her to do so without her sister's knowledge? Well, that's just difficult to conceive."

Leroy sprang up from his seat on the sofa chair that he'd been sitting in across from Reverend Perkins, his fingers were clenched into a tight ball at the end of his arms, which rested at sides. "You saying you know my wife better than I do? You saying she wouldn't do the things I said she's done? You calling me a liar?"

The reverend wasn't much smaller than Big Lou, and Leroy knew he'd be foolish to believe Reverend Perkins to be a candy ass because of his religious beliefs. It was just as foolish as anyone thinking that because Big Lou enjoyed intimacies with men, he'd be less of a force in hand-to-hand combat. But the reverend's comments had insulted his honor, and that sort of insult demanded justice. "Are you calling me a liar?" Leroy repeated in a threatening tone.

When Reverend Perkins had been knocking men twice the size of Leroy Blackman off their feet, driving them into the ground with such force they'd be sore for days after the initial impact, he'd been the sort of man who would have met Leroy's perceived attack, fighting posture, and threatening tone with an aggressive stance of his own. When crowds cheered, "Ike, Ike, Ike!" their chants had caused him to feel like a gladiator in the arena with thousands of Roman citizens applauding him for the violence and destruction he'd provided as entertainment. The man he'd been would have stood and met Leroy Blackman's threat with such great force that Leroy wouldn't have known what had hit him; he'd awaken like those men who attempted to halt his charge on the gridiron, wondering what freight train had run them over.

"Mr. Blackman I didn't mean to insult you. Neither have I come to your home for a fight. I've come out of concern for two members of my congregation, one being your wife and the other being her sister."

Leroy raised his tightly balled fist inches from his chest, and he placed his left leg behind his right. Reverend Perkins noticed that even in a boxer's stance, Leroy wasn't taking any steps closer. *He is bluffing,* Reverend Perkins thought. *Posturing just like an animal when it's trying to appear aggressive in order to fend off a threat, but it has no real ability to defend itself beyond the exaggerated display of strength and courage.* The pretense was what caused Reverend Perkins to realize that Leroy Blackman was exactly what Leroy has accused Perkins of referring to him as. He was a liar who was defending himself and pretending not to be one. The display, the loud talking, standing with his fist balled, his body poised to strike—it was nothing but a ruse, a means to cause anyone attempting to evade his space, from looking deeper into the story he was telling. He meant for people to stay clear of trying to discover the truth. "Because look at me, my balled fist, my angry visage. I'll hurt you if you push me," his behavior said. But in truth, Leroy wasn't the dangerous man that he was portraying, or so the reverend believed.

"Mr. Blackman I believe I've heard and seen enough to know that something in your home isn't as it should be. If I can't speak with your wife, and if you can't tell me where to find her, I'm afraid I'll have to go to the authorities myself."

Leroy used his fists to beat himself, hitting his skull with rights and lefts. They weren't powerful blows but had enough force that later he'd probably have a headache from the self-inflicted punishment. "She left! She left me for another man. How many ways can I tell you the same story? You don't know her like I do. Her own sister don't know her. I sleep with the woman, day in and day out, for eight years. I think I know her better than you and her damn, plump sister." He paced around the living room, moving back and forth like a caged tiger. "Okay, I'll call her. I'll dial her cell, and if she answers, you can ask her for yourself!" he said.

Leroy did pick up his cell phone, but he had no intention of dialing his wife's number. He was thinking about what the man in black had said to him at the crossroads. "Pick up the phone when you need me, and I'll answer. Just ask for Moody Johnson."

Leroy placed his cell to his ear, feeling silly about it because he hadn't dialed a number. Still, he placed it there, waiting to hear a ring or voice. "Hello?" he said. "Are you there, Moody, Mr. Johnson?"

"Hello, friend." Leroy jumped, startled by the voice coming from his cell. "How can I assist you?"

Leroy spoke with as much code as he could, pretending as if he was speaking with his wife so that the Reverend Perkins wasn't alerted to the fact that he wasn't. "Shelly, your pastor is here. He thinks I've done something to you, harmed you or something. So does your sister, on account of you not returning no calls. I read your letter, but I can't show no one on account of I burned it. Yes, that was a stupid thing to do, but I need you to speak with the pastor Perkins, let him know I ain't telling no lies."

First there was only a sinister laughter coming from the other side of Leroy's cell, a joviality that someone had over a thing that wasn't really funning, like someone laughing while watching kittens burn, or seeing a man get run over by a train, or witnessing the world burn to ashes. It was the laughter of a depraved individual who was overjoyed by the pain and suffering of others.

"Leroy, I only see one way out of this for you. That reverend isn't going to ever believe you, and unlike Sissy, when the good Reverend Perkins goes to the cops, they'll respond to him. Soon they'll be knocking on your door."

"He's a big fella. I don't know if I can take him," Leroy mumbled softy so Reverend Perkins couldn't hear.

"Tell him you've lied, that your wife is in the bedroom, that you struck her after that argument and are afraid you've gone too far." Leroy nodded his head up and down, watching the expression on Reverend Perkins's face as he does. "He'll be distracted enough for you to smash his head in with that solid iron lamp on the cocktail table." Leroy was astonished that Moody Johnson knew that he had an iron lamp on his cocktail table. But then, he was sure Moody Johnson knew a great deal more about a ton of things Leroy had no earthly idea of how Mr. Moody Johnson knows so much. He didn't mull over the question in his head instead of trying to figure out the impossible he simply responded by saying okay.

The Reverend Perkins never saw Shelly—or for that matter, Lana Monroe. All he saw when he opened the bedroom door and stepped inside of Leroy Blackman's bedroom was an unmade bed, the dresser, and the nightstands that Shelly had purchased, along with the other items that she thought would provide a peaceful resting place. He heard the cracking sound in his ears, like someone had used a hammer to break a coconut, or how football helmets sounded when men collided into one another. When he'd fallen to his knees and another cracking sound exploded like a baseball being hit with a wooden bat, he hadn't been conscious and didn't hear it. Several more explosive cracks echoed through the house, followed by a few mushy, smacking noises like someone pounding against a wet surface.

When Leroy finished bashing in Reverend Perkins's skull all the way down to his soft gray matter, he dropped the iron base of the lamp and stared up at Lana Monroe, who sat up on the edge of his bed. "Wow, you sure whacked him good. Don't think he'll be speaking with any cops—at least, not any living ones." She had a grin on her face as if she enjoyed the display of violence; it was an eerie, depraved expression that seemed to him oddly similar to what a face might look like if it belonged to someone who might find it funny to see kittens burn, or a man get run down by a train, or the world burned to ashes. He shook his head and dismissed the thought that Lana Monroe and the man in black may be derived from the same evil, unnatural energies.

Lana helped him clean the mess of what had poured from Reverend Perkins's skull, and she promised to help load his bulk into the back of his Olds. It had been Lana's suggestion to take Reverend Perkins's body to the crossroads instead of hauling him to the Mississippi, as Leroy had done with Shelly's corpse. "He won't be found there," she'd said. "No one will come looking for him in a place that no one knows exists." Leroy nodded in agreement, and together they went about the detailed work of making evidence of Reverend Perkins disappear.

5.

Forty-eight hours, give or take a few hours, was how long it took for the Sunflower sheriff's department to respond to reports of two of its missing citizens. Sheriff Andy Collins ordered two of his deputies to go to Leroy Blackman's home and retrieve him for questioning concerning the whereabouts of his wife and to see whether he knew anything about the missing Reverend Perkins. He gave orders for another two of his deputies to look for any clues near or around the Blackman home that may provide physical links to a crime.. He wouldn't be able to search Leroy's home without a warrant unless Leroy provided him permission, which he doubted the man would. Sheriff Collins figured if Leroy could make two people disappear without a trace, then he had to have a bit more than air filling the space between his ears. He was sure Judge Akins would provide him with the needed search warrant, but until then, he'd have to stay clear of Mr. Blackman's domicile.

Leroy sat in the only interrogation room at the Inverness police headquarters. The space was a four-walled concrete room not much larger than a walk-in closet. It had only one way in and out, and there was no one-way glass for officers to study a suspect's reaction to being placed in a room before being interrogated. Small-town municipalities didn't have the budgets of larger cites in order to purchase the fancy technology to help in solving crimes or investigating criminals. Collins was sheriff of Sunflower County, and the city of Inverness (population 1,019) consisted of about equal number of African American and Caucasian citizens. Sheriff Collins didn't concern himself too much with the comings and goings of the Caucasian population; Mississippi was still one of the most segregated states in the country, and the Delta region drew a line between the black and white races more than any other location in the state. He was sheriff, but his responsibility was mostly policing the black population, leaving the law enforcing of white citizens to white officers.

The ten to fifteen murders that took place in Sunflower County in any given year consisted of what might be considered the accidental type, where two men would get into an argument and their disagreement erupted into a fistfight. One fella would decide a beer or wine bottle would give him the advantage in a scuffle, and he'd swing the bottle wildly, blindly connecting with his fellow combatant's skull in that exact spot hunters referred to as the kill zone, the place on the body that would kill a man if hit with enough force. Every year, along with someone getting hit with a beer bottle in a drunken scuffle, at least one kid playing with his father's guns would pull a trigger and kill a sibling or friend. Then there were the hunting accidents, where some old boy drunk on moonshine, far too intoxicated to be behind the wheel of a vehicle or to be toting a loaded rifle, thought for sure the figure he saw lurking around in the bush had been a deer and not a man. The murders that accrued in the small towns of Sunflower County weren't of the cold-blooded type that happened in places like Jackson, New York, or Chicago. There weren't any criminal investigations or hunts to find a killer. That was why Andy was being diligent in his investigation into Leroy Blackman's missing wife and the sudden disappearance of Reverend Isaiah Gerome Perkins.

Andy had left Atlanta after twenty years of witnessing some of the most egregious crimes one human could commit on his own kind. He'd burned out as a big-city detective and couldn't take any more of the death, murder, and inhumanity. But he'd been a cop all his life, and he couldn't think in any other way. Attempting to learn a new trade at his age would be like trying to teach an old hound new tricks. When he'd been young, like so many wide-eyed adolescents beginning to feel themselves, the hair on their testes and chest starting to sprout, Andy couldn't wait to leave the small town where he'd grown up. Andy grew up not too far from Inverness; he'd spent his youth in Greenville, Mississippi, all eighteen years of it. Then he'd visited the recruiting office and joined up for four years in the army. He'd been eighteen, mean, lean, and dumber than a rock. But the army taught him how to be a man and provided him with the necessary mental tools to have a life when his tour of duty ended. Andy liked the structure and discipline of the police force; the rules and duties and dedication to the job didn't feel so different from the four years he'd spent with the army. Being an officer of the law felt natural, and for twenty years of his life, he'd been a good cop.

Eventually, he couldn't deal with the pressure and stresses of being a cop in a large city. The wife he'd loved for fifteen years divorced him. His children didn't speak to him. His career, the only thing he still had, turned his day-to-day into a living nightmare. He hadn't planned on being a cop again. He'd returned to the one place he'd fought so hard in his youth to get away from: the slow, isolated, boring life in a small town. He wanted to put behind him the things he'd seen and done as a cop in Atlanta, and he hoped the fresh air and isolation of a small town could cleanse him of the dirty living and the conditions of Sodom and Gomorrah from large cities, where it seemed everyone couldn't help but get a little tainted by in living in such a sinful environment. He'd stepped into the sheriff's role five years ago. Most of his job consisted of writing tickets, arresting moonshiners, and ordering kids to clean the graffiti they'd made. His biggest crimes were the few accidental murders per year that didn't need any investigating to solve.

He sat in his office chair behind a mostly empty desk, rubbing his hands over his receding hairline. Leroy Blackman was causing the stress of being a cop to return. *Damn*

Leroy Blackman to hell, he thought. Then he rose from his chair with a clipboard and pen in his hand and headed toward the interrogation room.

6.

Andy had been around enough criminals and liars in his lifetime to know when a man was not telling him the truth. It didn't take him hours of questioning to uncover that Leroy Blackman was guilty, but of what, Andy still needed to discover. If Shelly Blackman and possibly Reverend Perkins didn't turn up alive, then Leroy may be guilty of their murders.

"Mr. Blackman, you understand that from my perspective, not knowing either you or your wife …" Andy paused to look down at his notes. "Shelly. Your story is that Shelly picked up and left without so much as taking time to pack her belongings, including leaving behind a 2014 Volkswagen of which I've learned she is very fond." Andy lowered his eyes toward the clipboard on the stainless steel table that created a divide between him and Leroy Blackman. He knew exactly what was written in his notes, but reading from written statements caused the guilty to feel uncomfortable, knowing that their words had been written. Somehow, their words being placed on paper gave them more permanence, and the lasting statement could be used as historical record. As Sheriff Collins pretended to read from his notes, he noticed that Leroy appeared bored more than worried, as if sitting in a police station interrogation room and being asked questions concerning his missing wife and the Reverend Perkins was as about uninteresting as listening to the details described by an insurance salesman as he explained why one needed the extra coverage on a life insurance policy. Leroy was sitting impatiently, like he was waiting for the questioning to end so he could continue whatever he'd been doing before the cops interrupted his afternoon.

He's guilty, Andy. He's done killed them both, his wife and the Reverend Perkins. Andy's head whipped, turning over his right shoulder and then his left, toward the entrance of the interrogation room. Of course there was no one there. He only thought there'd be someone on account he'd heard the voice, and he hadn't heard it in such a long time that he'd believed it had come from some other source. But now, after seeing that no one had entered the room, he knew the voice had been that of the Detective, the hawk and bloodhound combination with an ability to find clues with eyes or sense of smell, tracking with those unordinary, gifted talents the guilty, innocent, or dead.

Andy had come to refer to his extrasensory ability to solve mysteries of the most unordinary and difficult crimes, the voice that spoke to him when his own mind couldn't see or sense past the few facts and inconsequential evidence, as the Detective. The voice could determine whether a story someone was telling was leading down a trail of truth or lies.

The Detective could see it in Leroy's eyes, in his body language; he could hear it in the man's voice. Lies were like the energies of spirits that could be sensed by those sensitive to the presence of phantoms. The Detective had sensitivity to lies. Leroy didn't know it yet, but the Detective relayed his thoughts. *He doesn't know it, but his days of walking around as a free man are soon to come to an end.*

7.

Leroy didn't—or rather, couldn't—see it. He was just a down-on-his-luck man. What had Shelly referred to him as? An alcoholic son of a bitch. Yes, that was what he was deep down, where it counted, he was not even a man; he was just an alcoholic, a booze hound, a good-for-nothing drunk.

Mr. Moody Johnson had known that, had figured that much out the moment he'd laid eyes on Leroy Blackman. Moody took pride in being able to figure people out, learning what it was that made certain people tick—those mechanisms like the inner workings of a clock, tiny pieces of moving parts that were the gadgets that propelled them in their decisions. Even the best of them were in a constant race with time: the time they'd lost, or the lack of future time they had to do this or that. Time wound down and would eventually run out. Time was the enemy of dreams and haunted men with the memory of moments that had passed and were forever lost. Moody had been quietly and patiently waiting in the shadow of hope that all men, like Leroy Blackman, used as fuel to get past the feelings of loss and despondency, which eventually caused them hope to lose illumination, dulling the glow of hope. Then Moody would rise and claim ownership of body, mind, and soul.

Moody understood what drove men, the one thing they valued above all others—more than love, fame, or riches? Most confused the wanting of physical and emotional desires, which were insignificant without time, without enough hours, days, or years to enjoy those pleasures. Moody noticed what Leroy had not; Moody had been listening, making sure Leroy didn't say anything stupid. In the end, Leroy would pay what was owed, but Moody was not finished having his fun. Leroy was a human wrecking ball, crumbling the lives of men and women. Leroy would kill again. He would take as many lives as necessary in order to keep the time he'd been given to seek his fortune and fame. Moody enjoyed the bloodshed, the pain and suffering of others; it allowed him to feel relief from his own misery.

Moody hadn't thought much of Sheriff Andy Collins at the start. He saw at the beginning a man who wore the years of his pains on his face, identifying his emotional suffering like boxers' scars identify the physical battles they had in the ring. Those mental or physical wars could damage a man, causing him to appear older in body, mind, and spirit than his true age.

When Andy Collins had first opened the door and entered the interrogation room, Moody thought he looked like a punch-drunk boxer; he appeared bewildered, confused, and dazed. His emotional struggles caused his metal state to resemble a pugilistic boxer who'd taken one too many blows to the head. Moody guessed the sheriff's age to be somewhere between late fifties or early sixties, but he could be wrong. He was like fighters who'd fought one too many rounds, whose broken noises and the scar tissue that formed over numerous places where the skin had been cut and stitched back together, walked as if they were in a constant state of pain. These men were aged more than their true years. The Sheriff may be ten or fifteen years younger than his physical appearance.

Moody had almost dismissed Andy as a threat because of what he appeared to be. Moody had almost not noticed that Andy's senses were keener then he'd first believed them to be. *He almost saw me,* Moody thought. *He looked past the empty, mindless shell housing Leroy Blackman and he almost saw the strings. He almost noticed fingers moving like appendages gliding over the keys of a piano, striking ivory to produce sounds in the same way fingers controlled the strings attached to Leroy Blackman.* For a few seconds Andy and Moody had locked eyes, and when they had, Moody had seen someone else: not the emotionally drained, balding man with dull brown eyes and weathered skin that looked like old leather boots. He didn't see a man who looked physically and emotionally twenty years beyond his actual age. He didn't see the pugilistic fighter who'd taken one too many blows to his head. After Moody took another, deeper look, the weakness that he'd thought would prevent the sheriff from being a worthy adversary suddenly made him seem rugged and strong. Moody had no idea he'd been staring into the eyes of the Detective, the street-smart, emotionally and physically tough persona that had allowed Andy to survive for twenty long years as a cop on the streets of Atlanta. Even Andy hadn't realized that the Detective had travelled with him from Atlanta to Mississippi, lying dormant and waiting for the time when he was needed

Moody recoiled. He hated the sudden fear, and he hated Andy Collins for causing him to feel such weakness. He'd been caught off guard, was all? He'd recover, gain his strength. When he did, he'd be sure to make Sheriff Andy Collins pay for causing him to feel weak, to feel human.

8.

Andy hadn't like what he'd seen in Leroy Blackman's eyes. They'd been the eyes of a killer, a man without remorse. Andy knew if Leroy Blackman had to kill again, he would. Andy wanted to throw the man in a cell, keep him locked away from good, law–abiding folks. But he couldn't lock a man away on suspicions, even if deep down he knew that what he felt was correct, and that locking Leroy Blackman in a cell for the entirety of his life would be the right thing to do. Andy couldn't even hold him any longer because after the questioning, he has no concrete proof that would hold up in a court of law.

"You're free to go, Mr. Blackman," Andy said. Speaking the words was like chewing glass. "But I don't want you leaving town without informing the sheriff's department." He knew even this threat couldn't hold water any more than a jug with a hole in it could.

Leroy didn't say a word; he simply rose from his seat and walked out of the interrogation room without looking back over his shoulder. He kept his eyes ahead of him all of the way to the front door of the police station until he reached his vehicle that he'd driven as he'd followed the deputies to the station earlier that afternoon. The only thing on his mind was returning home to practice his horn. Playing it would make him forget about Shelly, Reverend Perkins, Sissy Cousins, his visit to the sheriff's office, and whatever else would follow. *Would you sell your soul for it?* He heard the question being asked in his mind, and after all that had happened, his answer was still yes.

"Man creates both his God and his devil in his own image. His God is himself at his best, and his devil himself at his worst." —Elbert Hubbard

"You are of your father, the devil, and you want to do the desires of your father. He was a murderer from the beginning."

"For we wrestle not against flesh and blood, but against principalities, against powers, against the rulers of the darkness of this world, against spiritual wickedness in high places."

SISSY'S DEVIL

1.

LEROY HADN'T NOTICED the gray Ford pickup pull out of the parking space a few seconds after he'd steered his Olds from the spot where he'd left it in the visitors' parking lot of the Indianola sheriff's department. He was too busy in his own thoughts. Although Moody Johnson was always present in Leroy's mind, for now he'd receded to the place of shadows, and so he'd not seen the pickup either. The pickup followed behind Leroy, staying two hundred feet away from the rear bumper of the Olds, mimicking each of his turns and his speed.

When he'd left the police station, Leroy had turned right instead of taking the left turn, which would have led him in the direction of Inverness. He'd decided that he'd first make a pit stop. He'd not had a drink since this morning and booze in his tank is near empty. He'd arrived at the sheriff's office around three that afternoon and sat alone in the interrogation room for another hour—time to sweat out whatever guilt he may be feeling, he supposed. Then after he'd been made to wait with his own thoughts for company, Sheriff Collins himself, not a deputy but the boss man, had come to interrogate him. Their back and forth had lasted for nearly three hours, and most of their conversation had consisted of Sheriff Collins asking the same questions in numerous different ways, with Leroy providing the same answers to each of them. The cat-and-mouse game ended, and the afternoon had rolled forward to early evening. Ruby's place wouldn't be packed; there weren't as many early evening drinkers as there were late-night boozers, which in his current state of mind suited him fine.

Perhaps Lana Monroe would make an appearance. He hadn't seen or heard from her since the business with Reverend Perkins. He figured Lana was lying low, which was a smart thing to do until the coast was clear. He'd thought about paying Lana a visit at the boarding house where she'd been renting a room, but then he decided against it. He worried the cops, or someone like Sissy Cousins, may be watching his every move. He kept much as he could to his normal routine: waking, drinking, going to work, returning home, and drinking a bit more to take off the edge of a hard day's work. Then he'd practice his horn, sitting on his bed with his hands wrapped around the soft brass, his mouth pressed against the smooth metallic surface of the mouthpiece. He'd blow into his horn until his lips were numb from the constant pressure and his lungs burned from the strain of pushing excessive amounts of air through his respiratory system.

He'd made it through the week and had started to believe perhaps he'd also make it past having to answer questions concerning his missing wife and Reverend Perkins. But before the week ended, before his weekend had a chance to begin, deputies arrived at his home fifteen minutes after he'd arrived home from eight long hours cleaning catfish guts off the floor and wherever else they landed. He'd not had an opportunity to dull that edge sharpened by spending hours of his day engaged in an activity that he wouldn't wish on his worst enemy. That was the reason he'd taken the right instead of the left turn that would have taken him home. He needed a drink, and although the crowds at Ruby's wouldn't start pouring in for another two or three hours, the drink would provide him with the ingredients needed to dull that blade of frustration that caused him to lose sleep and was the reason for his headaches and the knots in his shoulders.

Leroy steered his Olds onto the dry dirt clearing that surrounded Ruby's place. He parked in an empty space that wasn't identified as a parking space by the usual yellow or white lines; patrons of Ruby's parked wherever they found enough space to plant four wheels. He walked toward the entrance of the club, and as he did, he noticed Big Lou guarding the entrance in his usual absent way, where he seemed more concerned with having conversations than paying attention to details. Leroy thought a man could be wearing a bomb vest above his jacket, carrying an assault rifle in one hand and a few grenades in the other, and Big Lou would simply wave him in.

Leroy received a few side-eyed stares, and he noticed folks whispering to one another as he walked. Even Big Lou did his best to conceal his thoughts, but Leroy could tell everyone else had heard of the rumors. Each of the folks, including Big Lou, had heard about the tales, and Leroy knew gossip had already spread. Most folks had already come to their own conclusions concerning the reasons why Shelly was missing and what had happen to Reverend Perkins

"Hey, Big Lou." Leroy spoke first, attempting to break the silence that was solid and cold as ice.

"Hey, my man Leroy," Big Lou responded, but not with his usual exuberance. "You're getting an early start on it tonight." Leroy knew by Big Lou's comment that he was asking about the reasons behind Leroy arriving at Ruby's just after the sun had set, before the real partygoers made an entrance.

"Been a fucked-up day," Leroy offered.

"Yeah, know what you mean. Some days you're the hound, and other days you're the coon," Big Lou responded. Big Lou slapped hands with a tall, brown-skinned man who walked past him and through the entrance of Ruby's. "No matter what day it is, if you're a coon or if you're a hound, one thing's for sure: you gotta wake up running." Big Lou had unusual insight concerning how to deal with good and bad days.

Leroy snaked his way past Big Lou in a way that the man's leering eyes could not clearly follow his path. Then before he entered, he decided to pause, ask big Lou a question that if anyone would have information about the comings and goings of patrons, and could answer his inquiry it would be Ruby's door man.

"You wouldn't have happened to notice if that young, light-skinned Creole girl has showed up this week?" he asked Big Lou.

The skin between Big Lou's eyes wrinkled, as if he was concentrating or confused about something. "Light-skinned Creole girl?"

"Yeah the light-skinned Mona Lisa I walked out of here with a couple of weeks ago." Leroy used the slang "Mona Lisa" to indicate he was referring to a rare, one-of-a-kind, beautiful woman.

Big Lou stood frozen, looking like one of those wax Neanderthal replicas one would see in the museums—creatures that didn't develop enough brains to survive the evolving world. Then he looked as if he'd just gotten the butt of a joke that had been too complicated for him to understand, his dimwitted mind having to repeat the punch line over and over until finally getting what more developed thinkers already had comprehended. He started to chuckle.

"What in the hell's so funny?" Leroy was trying to very hard to remain composed, but he had already been crapped on today, and he didn't need another turd adding a stench to the order still clinging to him. "Look, man. Either you seen her or you haven't. No reason for all of the laughing and carrying on." Leroy hoped his calm, diplomatic tone would keep the volcano within him from erupting.

"Yeah, Leroy. I seen the light-skinned Creole girl. But I didn't know that's what they're calling it now," Big Lou said, still chucking as if Richard Pryor or Eddie Murphy was standing across from him and telling one-liners.

"Calling what? What you talking about, man?" Leroy said louder than he meant, causing a few heads to turn in his direction.

"You walked out with a hell of a light-skinned Creole that night. Had you staggering and mumbling to yourself. You left her over there," Big Lou said, pointing to the right side outside the wooden wall of Ruby's juke house. "She was all over that there wall—Mona Lisa, that is. I guess Ruby didn't know your light-skinned Creole was going to be a masterpiece. Suppose if she had, she wouldn't have had it hosed off and cleaned away." Big Lou's chuckle turned into a full-blown, stomach-clinching laugh.

Leroy now stood like the dim-witted caveman he'd accused Big Lou of being, trying to catch up to present events with a brain that was stuck in a slower, more basic period of time. "You telling me you didn't see me leave here with a young woman?" he asked, uncertain now of his own recalling of events during his drunken night.

Big Lou's laughter eased down like an engine after a heavy foot raised up from the accelerator, until finally it slowed to a chuckle and then completely halted. "Leroy, you must have been drunker than I thought you'd been that night. I mean, I've heard of folks seeing pink elephants and blue monkeys, or whatever illusions that conjures in intoxicated minds. But I ain't never heard no one seeing a young Creole girl." Big Lou chuckled again, but this time it didn't last. He raised his giant paw and pointed a long, thick index finger in the direction of the wooden wall on the right side of Ruby's once again. "Your Mona Lisa, the Creole girl, whatever remained of her, got washed off the wall and cleaned away."

Leroy wanted tell Big Lou to go straight to hell that he was nothing more than an envious liar. But Leroy wasn't so sure whether Big Lou was that, so instead of calling him a liar, he silently walked past him and headed toward an empty bar stool inside Ruby's place.

2.

The waiting in itself wasn't what was causing Sissy to feel anxious. It was the combination of nervousness (a natural reaction to not knowing what would happen next) and her inability to console herself in her regular way when she felt anxiety over something. She'd normally reach into her glove compartment, where she always concealed a box of chocolate chip cookies or her beloved swiss rolls. If only she'd driven her own vehicle and had not relented to being a passenger in Jackson's Ford pickup. But Leroy may have recognized her Thunderbird because he'd seen it on numerous occasions. The likelihood that she and

Jackson could have followed him without being noticed was unlikely. They'd decided that Jackson—her younger half-brother, a child who came into the world as a result of her father's infidelity, the youngest of five children fathered by the man who had promised to love, cherish, and deny all women except for her mother, who managed to not only break his oaths but also was one-half responsible for creating physical manifestations in the form of bastard children who are living and breathing representations of his sins—would drive.

Jackson was the only boy. Then there were Sissy and her sister Shelly, along with the two other girls sired by Tommy Cousins outside of his marriage, totaling five offspring altogether. Jackson had been a rambunctious child, unruly and rowdy in every way a boy lacking in parental love and guidance could have been. Jackson's mother had killed a boyfriend and had been sent away to serve life behind the bars at Parchment Correctional Institution for Women. Jackson had been twelve when his mother became a prisoner of the state of Mississippi. Her new status caused her to lose custody of her six children, making them wards of the state—just as much prisoners as she herself had become.

Sissy had felt a desire to rescue Jackson. She wasn't sure whether the feeling had come from the emotional connection of having lost her mother at a young age, or from the fact that she and Jackson had the same blood running through their veins. Perhaps it had been a combination of both. She'd petitioned to the state of Mississippi that although she'd been only twenty at the time, she felt she could take care of Jackson better than the state. Jackson had come to live with her, and she'd attempted to raise him as best she could. But Jackson had an evil inside of him, and no matter how much love, praying, laying hands upon, or even punishment, nothing exorcise it from within him.

When Jackson had reached the age of fourteen, he'd been arrested for stealing and had been sent to the boy's reform school. By eighteen he'd graduated from petty theft to armed robbery, and that crime had placed him behind bars for two years at Parchment. He'd been in and out of prison—mostly in—over the past twenty-five years of his life. Sissy didn't ask any more about what he'd done; she didn't want to know. She simply prayed for him, visited him whenever he was locked away in that God-forsaken place, preached to him as much as he would listen, and hoped that someday the demon inside of him would be cast out by God's holy words.

Sissy had been on her way to pay Leroy Blackman a visit, and she'd brought Jackson along with her to do what holy men would not do. Men like Reverend Perkins, who now was missing as well. She couldn't help feeling guilty for the role she may have played in the events that led to his sudden disappearance. Reverend Perkins was a holy man, and Sissy knew one could not send a man of God into hell to fight a demon. Sometimes one had to fight evil with evil. But did she really believe that, or was she using that as an excuses so she could turn a blind eye to her true feelings? Sissy ignores the question concerning her reason for retrieving Jackson to deal with Leroy.

She and Jackson had been on the way to pay Leroy a visit when they'd discovered that he'd been requested by the Indianola sheriff's department for questioning. They'd parked outside of the sheriff's station, waiting for the result of Leroy's interrogation. Jackson had been adamant that Leroy would be released on account of the cops not having any real evidence against him, because they didn't have the dead bodies. Sissy had held faith that man's law, infused with God's righteousness, would prevail in getting the truth out of Leroy Blackman.

The waiting outside of the sheriff's station hadn't been as unbearable as the waiting now. They'd gone to McDonald's, and Sissy had ordered a Big Mac with extra cheese, an order of fries, an apple pie, a salad, and a large orange soda. The goodies helped with the anxiety of waiting and not knowing.

After what seemed like hours, Sissy watched as Leroy walked from the sheriff's department—no cuffs, no flashing lights of reporters trying to snap a picture of a killer, no shirt lifted over Leroy's guilty face while trying to shield his visage from onlookers. Leroy strolled from the sheriff's office a free man, steps like he hadn't a concern in the world.

"Told you so," Jackson said as he smiled in that same coy, dangerous way that he'd been doing since his youth. "We will do this my way. He might not break with the cops, but believe you me, he'll be begging to tell whatever secrets he's got when I get to asking. You can count on that." Jackson turned to face Sissy in order to read whether or not she believed him. He saw in her fear that she did.

Sissy couldn't recall if it had been her idea or Jackson's to follow Leroy home and do whatever was needed in order to discover what had happen to Shelly and Reverend Perkins. She stared out of the large front widow of Jackson's pickup; he'd reversed into a parking space about fifty feet from the front door of a place called Ruby's. Sissy had heard of Ruby's, a place of drinking, dancing to secular music, and fornication. She'd never come this near the walls of a juke joint, and it surprised her how much fear she had about the place. Leroy hadn't gone home, and it seemed he may not for quite some time. That feeling of having to wait without having something to fill her stomach and comfort her anxiety bothered her more than what Jackson would do once Leroy came out, and after they followed him home

3.

Lana Monroe made her entrance in the hours after he'd downed two drafts, a shot of Jack (the black label version), and half a mason jar of hundred-proof moonshine. The getting-drunk pace in which he downed his mixture of intoxicating drinks took him about an hour. His first thought had been to take her by the arm, and steer her across Ruby's small inner sanctum, the place for anyone who desired to drink away memories of a bad day, a relationship, or whatever else was keeping them from having a peaceful mind. He'd lead her by the crook of her arm to where Big Lou stood guarding the entrance, placing Lana directly in front of him—close enough that if he wanted to, he could reach down with one of his bear-sized paws and touch her face. But by the time Lana made her way to where he was sitting and nursing his remaining moonshine, he'd decided there was no point in parading the girl across Ruby's in order to prove that his Mona Lisa wasn't some drunken hallucination. Perhaps Big Lou was more of a girly man than he had suspected; that was the only reason Leroy could come up with to account for any red-blooded American man not taking notice of Lana Monroe. *What does it matter?* He thought. *It makes no difference to me if Big Lou believes Lana exists. I don't have anything to prove to him.* Was it that, or was it something else?

He dismissed this thought and raised the mason jar toward Lana so that she'd know he'd noticed her. He downed the jar—enough liquor to leave an average drinker facedown, his lips kissing the stained-wood bar and his mind oblivious to the ridiculous spectacle he was making of himself. But not Leroy. His tolerance had been built up over years of drinking, and his body had learned how to overcome the effects of alcohol. He could consume amounts that would send any other fella into a coma.

"I didn't come here to drink with ya, Chocolate," Lana replied when he offered to buy her a drink. She'd come out tonight, she said, to make sure that in his drunken state, he didn't begin to share information that wasn't meant to be known by anyone outside of her and Mr. Moody Johnson. Leroy felt a bit offended that Lana believed he needed a babysitter but if he was going to have one, then he supposed having one who looked like Lana Monroe made it okay.

Ruby's never did get packed. The Monday through Thursday crowd wasn't ever as large as the weekend patrons that began their incursions away from the mundane routines of everyday life on Friday evening, using alcohol to cloud the memories of a long, uneventful weeks, getting drunk enough so that a shield of intoxication guarded against the miseries of everyday life.

Leroy was at most two drinks away from his tolerance level, the point of no return when he'd end up face first on the bar rail or on the floor. He decided to pass on the one or two drinks that would tip him over the edge. He'd leave now, while he was still in possession of his motor skills. "Lana, let's get outta here," he said with a noticeable slurring. He'd drunk enough now so that he couldn't remember his visit to the sheriff's office or his worrying that

Andy Collins may be on to him. The booze made all of his thoughts peaceful and cheerful. He stumbled as he stood from the bar stool and placed his feet on solid ground. "Whoa!" he exclaimed like a man climbing into a saddle and grabbing the reins of a mare that suddenly galloped out of control. "I got it," he added as he waved away Lana's outstretched hand. Leroy balanced himself and slowly moved forward, placing one foot in front of the other like a man walking a tightrope hundreds of feet above ground level.

He staggered past Big Lou, giving him a winner's grin—the one football players had for the cameras after they'd won the championship game. Big Lou simply gave him a strange stare, which Leroy didn't notice.

"I can drive," Leroy interjected before Lana protested. After he stated his claim, she didn't suggest otherwise. He fumbled with his key, closing one eye in order to focus his sight. Then he inserted the key into the ignition and dropped the Olds into gear. It lurched forward, jerking like a kid in a last-period classroom, trying to fight the effects of exhaustion. He woke the Olds enough to get it moving at a pace that was consistent. He'd arrive home in about half an hour. Perhaps when he got home, he'd play a few tunes on his trumpet for Lana. She had said she liked the way he played, and perhaps if she liked his playing enough, the sweet music emitting from it may entice her in a sexual way. Probably not, but one never knew. Women were a bit fickle. *I probably can't get it up any way—not with all the booze in my system.*

While drunk behind the wheel of his Olds and feeling good about himself and his future, once again Leroy didn't notice the gray pickup that had been parked at the sheriff's department creep out from a concealed space at Ruby's.

Sissy jerked, startled from her sleep by the roar of Jackson's pickup as the old Ford's engine rumbled from a dormant state, sounding like an angry lion giving a menacing, warning bellow to detour any threats near its borders. She'd fallen asleep sometime between Leroy entering Ruby's and his departure.

"He's on the move," Jackson relayed the news to her, never turning from the tail lights that marked Leroy as his prey.

Sissy wiped her eyes. The dreamy images of sleep were still present, blurring her focus of her surroundings. *What time is it? How long have I been sleeping?* Sissy asked these questions to herself, knowing that asking such a simple question would only produce a response similar to a shrug in her mind.

"How long have we been waiting?" Sissy asked, looking out through Jackson's dirt-stained side window and into the gray clouds and starless darkness of the night. She tried her best to gauge the hour from the degree of darkness.

"He was in there for nearly four hours, drinking enough until he either ran out of cash or had reached his limits." Sissy saw the corners of Jackson's mouth curve into what she supposed was a smile, but he clenched his teeth when exposing his ivories, like he'd done as a young boy. The smile on Jackson's face always made her feel uncomfortable; it didn't appear genuine in a true definition of what a smile was supposed to represent. Even when he'd been a boy, small and fragile and seemingly in need of protection and love, Sissy had been aware of the wildness within her half-brother, a beastlike quality that caused her to realize he'd be a dangerous adult.

Sissy, you're foolish too. Delusional just as much as those folks believing they can raise tigers or pythons and that, because at one point the animals had been small and helpless, they wouldn't later grow into the beasts they'd been designed to become. The voice in her head spoke like the voice of God, and Sissy listened. She knew the voice, God, was warning her, hoping that forethought would intercede and prevent her from making a poor decision leading to costly consequences.

Jackson had managed to keep his focus for four hours, along with those other few hours before parking at Ruby's. Jackson's patience, and the endurance needed to complete any worthwhile project, was perseverance that he had never demonstrated, at least not in an attempt to succeed in tasks that promised to improve his life. He had somehow been able to awaken from some seemingly endless season of hibernation, a slumbering beast of provocation that Sissy had thought Jackson incapable of transforming into.

Sissy hadn't the time to ponder over the thoughts that God had placed in her mind, or her own. She watched from a distance as Leroy steered his Olds into a space fifteen or so feet from his front steps. She noticed that the interior of the house was dark—no indication of an angry or worried wife awake inside, sitting in a chair nervously and rocking back and forth, or angrily pacing the floor. Sissy was surprised by a thought: the hope she had in discovering her concerns were invalid. She'd mused that Shelly was okay, and that even Reverend Perkins's disappearance, although extremely odd, would be easily explained. Then both Shelly and the Reverend would be discovered, and later when she'd tell them of her worries, they'd share in a laugh.

The thought dissipated, losing shape and form, wiped away by truth like images formed by clouds that were blown away by winds. As she watched Leroy stumble from his vehicle and zigzag from right to left, causing the straight path to his front door to take more time to reach than it should, Sissy realized that her hope was no more solid than those cloud images. The truth was something bad had happen to Shelly, and Sissy had followed the trail of foulness and it has led her to the home of Leroy Blackman. .

"Wait here until I signal you that it's okay," Jackson said. She didn't protest. She'd loaded her weapon and pulled the trigger, and now Jackson was like a bullet shot from the barrel of a rifle, heading in the direction of its target.

"Hell is empty all of the devils are here." —Shakespeare

"Who am I?"

"I feel worse when I'm alone, because that's when the monsters in my head say hello."

VOICES IN MY HEAD

1.

LEROY SWUNG HIS screen door open, placed his key in the slot, and released the bolt to unlock his front door. Then he wave his free arm forward and low, as if he was taking a bow. Even in his drunken state, he thought he was a gentleman. "Welcome to my humble abode," he said as he allowed Lana to pass through the open doors first.

Leroy, you know you're completely insane. It was a voice that he'd not heard in a very long time, not since his mother had died nearly fifteen years ago. It relayed to him something he believed, at least in some way, down deep in his mind, in that abyss covered in so much darkness he could no more see clear thoughts than a man sinking into the depths of an ocean could see his own hands in front of his face.

"Mama, that ain't any way to talk about your son," he responded.

Leroy, you are going to fry like bacon on a skillet for the things you've done, the voice belonging to his mother said.

"Mama, get out my mind. You dead, Mama, and the dead don't have any say in things anymore."

There was a moment of silence, and then Mama had one final message for him. *You'll be dead soon too, Leroy. Soon you'll be in hell, getting poked in your rear by the devil's pitchfork and burning in the hot flames of hell's fires.*

"Don't ya be listening to her, Chocolate. She don't know nothin' bout nothin'," Lana said.

Leroy turned to face her because he was surprised Lana responded to what his mama had said. "Mama talks to you too?" he asked, confused.

"Dead can speak to the dead, Chocolate. Can hear them too," she responded. Leroy paused, staring at Lana, his eyes measuring her from head to toe.

"You really dead, Lana?"

"Well I'm somethin' like dead, Chocolate."

"What's that mean?" Leroy ask,

"Chocolate, I ain't dead, but I ain't alive either. Thought you'd already figured out that much."

Leroy stood in the threshold of his house, staring into the face of a women who'd just said she wasn't alive but wasn't dead either. He didn't know what that made Lana. He guessed some sort of zombie or vampire.

Leroy reached out to touch Lana to see if her flesh felt like the skin of a zombie or vampire. Was it cold and stiff? If the living dead felt anything like Shelly's corpse had felt, it'd feel similar to a pillow after having all of the goose down removed and replaced with cold water. He knew that feeling because of Shelly, when he'd touched her after her life force had departed her physical body. Shelly had felt like a heavy, cold, wet sack. He wondered now if he reached out and touched Lana, if he took her in his arms and lifted her off her feet, if she'd feel less buoyant and more like a sinking buddle of water-filled cotton bags that folks once laid their heads on at night.

When Leroy's fingers finally extended close enough to graze Lana, he was surprised at what he felt. Lana hadn't felt like a living person, but neither had she felt like one of the living dead. Lana didn't feel alive or dead. When he reached out to touch Lana, he hadn't felt anything at all.

2.

The drunken fool, Jackson thought after he observed Leroy standing in front of the entrance into his home, waving his left arm out in front of him as if he was a matador stepping aside while a charging bull passed inches from his body. The idiot hadn't even bothered to close the door behind him, leaving only a screen door as a barrier. It was no more capable of preventing anyone from gaining access into his home than the red cape could shield a man from two thousand pounds of charging flesh, bone, and muscle.

Gotcha, you lousy, wife-beating scum, Jackson thought as he gently pushed aside the screen door, attempting to not disturb the hinges so they'd not squeak. Jackson had no respect for men who beat wives or girlfriends; he viewed these men as spineless. Sure, he had backhanded a few women and gut-punched a few others, but he'd never struck a women out of personal feelings. His reason for using a heavy hand or foot had always been about business. He was what some might refer to as a pimp, but Jackson had never seen himself as a pariah dealing in the selling of sex.

Pariah—that was one of the dictionary words he'd learned during his many years of being educated in the prison system, reading books and learning meaning to words he'd never would have taken time to discover if not for being locked in a cell with nothing else to do except stare at walls to pass the time. He'd learned that a pariah was someone considered a social outcast. A simple pimp may be an outcast, which was why he didn't consider himself a pimp. He was simply a man taking advantage of whatever life placed in front of him. To Jackson, that made him just as much a part of the social fabric of the world as anyone else. Men like his brother-in-law, who beat women for no other reason than self-indulgence, getting excited from the control like an adolescent at his first sight of boobies, were the real pariahs. When Jackson had to strike women, it was not for his own pleasure; it was to get her moving or stop her from doing something she'd later regret. He disciplined them; it was to condition them for the life they'd be living, and it was no different than when a man took a whip to a mare's hide to get it to learn its place in the world.

Jackson reached toward his belt line, slowly extracting the Smith and Wesson Colt .45 from the space between his waistband and the brown leather belt supporting his loose-fitting, faded jeans. He was not surprised in his ability to sneak up on Leroy without being noticed; he'd been a talented cat burglar in his youth. "You're a late bloomer. Don't worry, Jackson. You'll catch up to your classmates in height and size soon enough," Sissy would promise whenever he came home upset because his classmates wouldn't pick him to play five-on-five basketball on the outdoor court behind Gentry High School. Sissy had been right about him being a late bloomer. He'd grown five inches and packed on thirty pounds of muscle between the ages of twelve and eighteen. Fortunately for him, he didn't have to wait on the sidelines until his body grew to a size where he'd be chosen for the five-on-five, full-court basketball games. His undersized physical form may not have been made for shooting a ball through a basket, but like Leroy Blackman, Jackson discovered other interests, a purpose for his life that aligned with his natural skills and abilities. He'd discovered his frame had been perfect for being hoisted up by larger boys high enough to reach windowsills then crawl through the narrow openings of windows or between spaces of bolted fences. His vocation as a cat burglar had been left behind when he'd grown too tall and wide to squeeze past gated fences or be lifted to a ledge. However, he maintained his stealth ability, allowing him to sneak up on someone without being heard or noticed. For a man of his stature, that was quite impressive.

When large cats hunted, it was said they could be silent as death. Jackson was four hundred pounds lighter than a six-hundred-pound king of the jungle, but for a man just under six feet tall with a body consisting of mostly lean muscle, his size was respectable.

3.

Leroy's focus had been on Lana Monroe, on the young woman who was and wasn't there, and on his mama, or at least her voice that came to him so clearly she could have been standing in the room a few inches from his ears. He was glad it had been only her voice; he didn't think he'd be able to handle seeing her ghost and simultaneously dealing with the fact that Lana Monroe may also be a ghost or some illusion he'd created in his own mind. *Leroy, you know you're completely insane,* Mama had said. He couldn't be sure whether his mother had returned from the death in order to provide him with a warning, because he'd been positive that Lana Monroe was a real, physical woman, and he'd been wrong about that.

Leroy, it's the moonshine, the Johnny Walker that has your mind jumbled and has you hearing voices in your head. It's the reason you reached out to touch Lana to feel her tight, young body, only to discover she's as void of substance as a gust of wind, a voice sounding very much like Mr. Moody Johnson proclaimed.

"Yeah, yeah," Leroy said aloud. "I'm drunker than I've ever been in my life, drunk enough to have fallen into an alcohol-induced delusion. Only I ain't seeing pink elephants or whatever else the booze causes the mind to imagine. Instead of the regular hallucinations, the booze has got me hearing voices and imagining Lana is transparent as rays of sunlight." He laughed as if he'd heard the punch line to a whopper of a joke. He would have continued laughing, howling out the fears and doubts that crept into his mind. But a mule—and he suspected it to be the same surly, stubborn beast that had first knocked him unconscious and had been the reason he'd awakened on that morning nearly three weeks ago with a throbbing frontal lobe and a monster of a headache—had the heavy hands of Mike Tyson, his knockout power bottled in a clear mason jar along with a mule's unmoving disposition. Mike's right hook concealed power, within a liquid fermented brew referred to as moonshine, smashed him in the back of his head, the pain stealing the cleansing feeling he had after a belly-emptying gaggle.

The aftereffects of boozing it up had never hit him so hard physically. Usually the journey from sober to inebriated was a slow, downhill jaunt where he was able to keep balance long enough to ensure he'd land someplace soft. But tonight, the combination of moonshine and Johnny Walker came out swinging at the sound of the bell, a flurry that first had him hearing voices and seeing women who weren't really there. *Lights out,* Leroy thought as he felt his knees buckle and noticed everything he gazed at was blurred, like he was looking at the world through a pair of prescription glasses belonging to someone with far less than the twenty-twenty vision of his own perception. He attempted to rise from the floor, but the mule hit him again hard on the back of his skull, and the drunken feeling sounded like a coconut being cracked by a hammer.

Then the mule shouted in an exclamation made by a man: "Stay the hell down, Leroy, or I'll bust you on your dome again!"

Anger pushed away the unconscious feeling. It was rage that allowed men to overcome in the final minutes before they would have succumb to effects of pain. It allowed Leroy to make one more effort to rise from his knees so he could at least say he went down fighting, that he didn't stay on his knees like a fella afraid to stand and fight.

Crack! This time the hammer spilt that coconut—not so much that all the insides came pouring out at once, but slowly like a small hole in a wall meant to hold back a river of water.

4.

Lights from inside of Leroy's home came on and went back out three times. *That's the signal,* Sissy thought. She turned the key, cranking the engine of her half-brother's pickup. Her chubby fingers gripped the steering wheel so tightly that her knuckles changed in color from light brown to red. *Of course you're nervous, Sissy. You have every right to be. You're in the devil's playground now, treading on ground made of brimstones and the bones of sinners.* Sissy thought the voice in her head might be the words of God, but she couldn't be sure anymore, because she'd crossed that line God marked as a divide from his people and Satan's minions, saying his children shouldn't crossover. She knew when one went over that line drawn in the sand, the line between words of saints and sinners, which one couldn't trust in the things one once believed. On the other side of the line, sinners practiced their trades, honing skills for that day when a child of God thought to crossover on account that she'd fallen from grace due to some great loss, causing the saved to question not only her own beliefs but God's guidance as well. Some fell so far that there wasn't a way of ever climbing back out of the pits of hell.

I'm doing what I'm doing for a just reason, Sissy replied to the voice that may or may not be the voice of God. Sissy didn't believe God would forsake one of his lambs if it crossed over into hell in order to save another lost sheep *isn't that the job of the saved? To help with the cleansing of the world by saving one soul after another?* Sissy asked the voice and her own doubting mind.

Is that what we've come to do? If that's the case, then why have we brought Jackson? Because we both know what he is. We know whose side he works for. We've known that since he was a small boy.

Sissy didn't respond because she had no words that would dispel the argument made by God, her own conscious, or whatever voices crept into the thoughts of people who crossed that line God had said not to step over. Instead of debating with whoever or whatever spoke to her, she focused on driving, ignoring all other musings.

Sissy sat behind the wheel of Jackson's truck, her knuckled grip the only thing keeping her from swooning and feeling completely numb. The physical pain steadied her and reminded her that this was real and not part of some nightmarish dream caused by her tendency to indulge in cookies and cakes that caused the stomach to get upset and the mind to stay busy long after she had shut her eyes, drifting to sleep into a world of silence and darkness. The tingling sensation of blood being removed from her hands and causing her knuckles to change color was enough consciousness awareness to cause her without a doubt to know she was in the material universe and not the abstract dream world of her nightmares. A nightmare would come to an abrupt end by her simply opening her eyes. But this was no dream. She'd come here to Leroy Blackman's home, and she'd brought with her a minion of Satan. She'd referred to her sister's husband as a devil throughout Shelly's eight-year marriage to him, and after learning more about his sinful ways, she'd become confident in her definition of what he was. But Leroy was nowhere near in ranking, if devils were ranked like angels of God. Sissy speculated that Satan himself, once one of the highest ranking angels in God's army, now was in command of his own battalion of scores of fallen angels and unrepentant men. Satan had started his journey in God's company, and there he'd learned his first lessons. Sissy believed the devil would command his army much in the same manner God had organized his own followers. She was sure devils and demons, and men who served both, fell into degrees of power and leadership determined by their ranks. She'd thought to acquire Jackson's assistance because of her belief that she could only fight fire with fire. But in Satan's order, Sissy was sure that Jackson was ranked well above the level of Leroy. She'd not released a man filled with dervish ways like she envisioned Leroy to be; in Jackson, she had opened up the gates of hell and allowed a five-star general in Satan's army loose in the house where her sister had made a home.

Shelly was probably hurt real bad or dead. Sissy hadn't really allowed herself to think much of that latter thought, until the Reverend Perkins went missing hours after he'd said he'd visit Leroy Blackman in order to get to the bottom of what had happened to Shelly. Her younger sister being with God was something that had crossed her mind more than the other thought brought about by images in her mind—the visions of Shelly bruised and bloody, gagged with a rag or handkerchief, her hands tied behind her back and her feet bound. She could be lying in a closet where Leroy had stuffed her away until her wounds healed, so he'd not have to suffer consequences for what he'd done to her.

You know your sister is dead. You know the Reverend Perkins is no longer among the living. And for some reason, the only person whom you can get to believe you is your devil of a step-brother, the voice said in her head. Sissy released the steering wheel, and blood rushed toward her extremities. Her fingers felt like they were being pricked by tiny, sharp needles.

The house lights were off now. Sissy wondered whether she was being responsible by continuing down a path that may lead her further away from what God desired and closer to contributing to Satan's designs. She'd come too far to turn back now. All she could do was cross over that line separating heaven and hell.

"I had a compulsion to do it."

"Even when she was dead, she was still bitching at me. I couldn't get her to shut up."

"I carried it too far, that's for sure."

THE MAN IN BLACK

1.

WOMEN, AS MUCH as men, feel a need to escape once the life they've been living begins to close in on them, and the space they're occupying begins to resemble a room the size of a prison cell, so small that it cannot expand enough in order to store all of their hopes and dreams. Men and women can feel like they're living behind bars when the world they reside in doesn't have the space for them to grow into the people they want to become. When the closed-in feeling becomes overwhelming and they feel like at any point they'll not be able to catch another breath, then before they allow the hopelessness and despair to suffocate them, they will use all of their remaining strength to escape whatever sort of cage life has place them within.

Sheriff Collins understood human nature. He had seen firsthand the atrocities committed by both men and women—heinous sins even those closest to them would swear on a stack of Bibles a spouse, sibling, or lifelong friend would never have the mind or heart to do, only to be shocked upon discovering someone they believed they'd known and loved could have committed such awful crimes. He'd seen it far too many times to say it couldn't happen.

Then why had he been losing sleep on account of Shelly Blackman? She may have done just as her husband had said; there wasn't evidence to prove otherwise. She was missing suspiciously during the same time Reverend Isaiah Perkins had chosen to disappear. Probably they both decided to skip town together, take a chance at happiness and love. Maybe their decision was a bit immoral, but he didn't police the spiritual rights and wrongs of men; he left that to men like Reverend Perkins and to God, if the heavenly father's chosen messengers lost their way in serving his flock.

If you believe that, then why are you up well past bedtime, driving around Inverness and interviewing anyone who may have seen Leroy Blackman or his wife around the time she'd gone missing? The Detective wasn't the type of fella to speak in parables. He came right out and said what he meant, and if anyone didn't like it, they could kiss him where the sun didn't shine. The Detective had noticed something within the eyes of Leroy Blackman when Andy had been interviewing him, something behind Leroy Blackmans dull, dark brown eyes. Andy (or more so the Detective) had seen what some said was the soul of men, and those eyes that were windows into the soul of Leroy Blackman had revealed a dark man—not simply a person who had bad thoughts or had committed horrible crimes, but a man who had transformed from human into something else. *He's the man in black,* the voice of the Detective said. *That illusive man who always manages to remain within the shadows, the one who destroys lives and never pays for his crimes because regular folks can't see past the human façade, can't look deeper into the evil see it for what it* is.

The men in black, the John Wayne Gacy's, Richard Ramirez's, Charles Masons, and Zodiac Killer, men who hungered for murder. Because of lust for taking lives, they were transformed into inhuman creatures that could only be described as men in black. This version of Andy Collins was a burned-out former detective whose only desire was to pass the years until retirement by serving his community. The current rendition of Andy Collins would have never noticed those minute clues that alerted any seasoned detective that a man was a monster in human form. The darkness within Leroy's eyes had awakened the Detective from hibernation, and now that he'd emerged from his long season of sleep, he was famished. The only thing that could sate his hunger was hunting, capturing, and locking away evil men.

Andy sat behind the wheel of his Jeep Cherokee, submerging himself completely into his alter ego. Only the Detective had single-minded focus, like a bloodhound that could locate a singular odor from within a tangled mixture of smells, following it until it discovered whatever or whomever it had been searching for. *Why don't we begin at Ruby's? Pick up a trail from there and see where it leads?* Andy thought the suggestion from the Detective seemed reasonable. Leroy spoke of spending his hours before his wife went missing getting drunk at Ruby's juke house. There had to be numerous patrons and employees that would have seen him coming and going, and they'd be able to provide a better, detailed description of his mental and physical condition.

Andy pulled up in front of Ruby's at 1:34 a.m., fifteen minutes after Leroy had made his exit from the illegal drinking and gambling establishment, where he'd been followed home by Jackson and Sissy Cousins. Andy would finish questioning remaining patrons and staff, the majority of which would be staying until Ruby's doors closed, sometime around five in the morning—near the same hour Leroy Blackman would have already been knocked to the floor, muttering incoherent words as blood poured from his thick skull before finally succumbing unconsciousness.

Andy walked up the path leading to Ruby's front door, a dirt passageway cleared by years of boots and shoes stomping out any turf that attempted to sprout. He saw the man nicknamed Big Lou standing guard, his large body almost expanding to the height and width of door. Andy noticed Big Lou retrieve a cell phone from his left pant pocket, lifting it to his ear and speaking into it as his eyes grew in size until they resembled the a fifties television character named Buckwheat, the only black kid who'd been a member of the gang on the *Little Rascals*. Big Lou's eyes stretched to their limits, the same as Buckwheat's when he viewed something that troubled or excited him. Ruby's doorman was a big ole' country boy who'd been in trouble with the law in his past but hadn't caused any criminal mischief in the years following his release from Parchment. Prison tamed the savagery in some men, but years behind bars released the primal beast in others.

Andy knew his presence would cause an avalanche, one beginning with a simple call from Big Lou's cell, which will cause human activity to move at the speed of falling snow and ice—exertions hoped to be enough to wash away evidence of illegal activity.

"Sheriff!" Big Lou announced, his greeting said so both Andy and whoever was listening on the other side of his cell could hear.

"Evening," Andy began, and then the corrected himself. "Morning, I mean." Staying up through the night threw off that internal clock, the one said to be biological, a part of humankind's instinctual behaviors. Andy couldn't help notices nervous glances in his direction. He was sure a few of the men and even women patronizing Ruby's were nervous due to his presence. *They're wondering if you've come to place cuffs around their wrists, lower them into the backseat of your Jeep, and escort them to a holding cell until a judge can see them on Monday to expedite a judgment on some past due warrant they've forgotten about.* Andy nodded slightly in agreement with the Detective's assumption, but not enough that anyone watching would notice.

Andy decided to cut to the chase. "I've come here to ask some questions of employees and customers: all of those present three Friday nights ago, between the time of ten at night and four in the morning."

Big Lou's head bounced around on his large shoulders like a bobble head folks kept on dashboards or office desk. *He's still anxious, afraid. You're the first of numerous lawman to show his face before twenty officers dressed in tactical gear ready to kick in doors emerge from concealment, yelling and screaming while ordering folks to drop to the floor as they raid the place.* Andy and the Detective were almost merged into one person, as they'd been during his years as a lead homicide detective. Back then, he'd needed the hawkeyed and bloodhound abilities of his alter ego to see and sniff out things a regular cop wouldn't notice.

"Well, Sheriff," Big Lou began slowly, like a kid not wanting to explain to his mother the reason he'd made a mess of his Sunday pants when the route home was a straight path down a paved road. Lou's large head kept bobbling around until his eyes were facing Andy again. "Sheriff, that'll be most everyone, give or take a few that are present now." Between the remaining patrons and Ruby's employees, there were twenty-three people in total.

Interviewing them all would be tasking, but Andy knew how to quickly eliminate a good witness from a bad one. "Well, I'd like to start asking your employees and then all those good citizens patronizing your little establishment a few questions. I'll need you to find me an isolated spot and then begin escorting each employee one by one to me. I'll start with the bartender, then the waitress, followed by the cooks, your remaining patrons, and lastly you." Andy didn't wait for Big Lou's response and moved toward the entrance of Ruby's. Big Lou did his best to quickly step away from his position in front of the door so the sheriff could enter.

2.

The amount of blood seeping from the back of Leroy's head had puddled around his skull as he lay face down on the floor, making gurgling noises in a mixture of his own sweat and body fluids, causing the swooning feeling to reassert itself. It was the same loosing of cerebral and physical equilibrium Sissy had while driving toward her sister's home with thoughts of discovering what has really happen to Shelly clear in her mind. Sissy had never been squeamish at the sight of blood, but she'd also never seen more than the amount that spilled from small cuts or scrapes. Her past experiences hadn't prepared her for the abundance of human fluids she saw now.

"I'm going to be sick," she announced, placing a hand over her mouth and turning away from Leroy's unconscious body. She vomited chunks of burger, bun, and what may or may not be blue cheese. "Jackson, you weren't supposed to kill him!" she muttered as she wiped remains of her regurgitated dinner from her lips and chin, using the sleeve of her loose blouse as a napkin.

"He ain't dead, but he may be wish he was when he wakes up," Jackson responded, obviously annoyed by Sissy accusation of having done something he was not supposed to have done.

Although Sissy doesn't want to, she turned and looked over her shoulder, down at the floor where Leroy was lying. She could see his back rising and falling. Now that the swooning feeling had passed, her equilibrium was steadied by the cleansing of the nerves in her stomach that the vomiting had provided. Sissy was able to see past the puddle of blood and the revolting feelings she had when she first laid eyes on Leroy on the floor, having lost more blood than it seemed possible for a man to lose and still be alive. Her clarity that had been blurred by the swooning feeling, which had not allowed her to focus on details, like Leroy's back moving up and down and those gurgling sounds caused by his breathing into his blood. These were indications that Leroy wasn't dead. But with so much blood already lost, it seemed to Sissy if Leroy wasn't dead yet, he may soon be.

"Shelly ain't here," Jackson abruptly announced, reminding Sissy of her more urgent reason for having come to her sister's home in the first place. It was a thought that had been push aside, if only temporarily, due to seeing so much blood.

Sissy realized in the minutes it had taken her to drive and then exit Jackson's pickup, Jackson has searched through the tiny house consisting of a bedroom, living room, and kitchen. In his search, he hadn't discovered any sign of Shelly.

Sissy and Jackson simultaneously lowered their eyes to Leroy, both of them thinking the same thing. If the head wound isn't plug soon, Leroy probably wouldn't survive. Sissy knew she'd have to bandage Leroy's wound to stop the blood loss, if she wanted to extract information about Shelly's whereabouts.

Jackson stood guard, peeking out of windows and pacing back and forth like a wild beast in a cage. He held his Smith and Wesson out in front of him every time he pulled back one of the curtains to peek out and survey the scene outside, holding his Smith and Wesson up in front of him like a lion folding back his gums to reveal sharp, dangerous canines. Jackson kept watch while Sissy did what she could to prevent Leroy from succumbing to his wounds. She swooned from the sight and the rusty iron aroma of blood and vomited one more time, but she was able to compose herself enough to get past her revulsion and find the gash where the leaking body fluid is passing through, and then patch the wound as best she could.

When Sissy began the task of bandaging Leroy, she ripped apart four white towels Jackson had retrieved from a drawer in the bedroom. Sissy's heart tore each time she heard the sound of the cotton fabric being ripped apart. These were her sister's towels. Sissy hoped they were not Shelly's favorites. The thought of using something precious to her sister in order to mend the skull of a foul, sinful man like Leroy Blackman made her sick to her stomach. But it was not the same weak, crumbling feeling she'd had when the sight and smell of blood had caused her stomach to loosen its grip on her dinner. The feeling in her belly caused by the thought of patching Leroy's wounds with her sister's favorite linen, cloths Shelly had probably used to dry her own body after a bath, came from a place of strength. The boiling of anger was hot like lava flowing deep beneath the earth's crust, and her feelings pushed toward the surface like hot rivers of molten rock simmering and reaching upward until it erupted. *I hope he dies. I want him to die,* a voice said to her—or was it her own voice? She was not sure, but either way, she didn't deny the truth in those words. After they got the information they wanted from Leroy, Sissy would enjoy knowing Leroy Blackman was no longer among the living.

"Hurry up with that. It ain't gotta be perfect. You aren't wrapping him to place him in no pyramid like he's a mummy or something," Jackson said as he continued to pace from one room to the next, peeking out of windows.

"I'm not spending more time needed. I just want to make sure he don't slip away, at least not before he tells me what he's done with my sister." Sissy paused, and then in a voice that didn't sound like her own continued with her thought. "After I get that information, Mr. Leroy Blackman can go straight to hell, where he belongs."

Jackson was halted from his pacing due to the sudden change in Sissy's words. Usually she spouted irritating and repetitive statements she'd lifted from the King James Bible. There were countless verses telling how men should be thankful, humble, and most of all forgiving. Sissy suddenly wasn't speaking as if her every independent thought had been taken from her and replaced with a hypnotic mantra that was given each time she heard or saw something not spoken of, or spoken against, within the pages of the Bible. Phrases such as "Praise the Lord," "In God's time," "Love thy enemy," "Turn the other cheek"—these were Bible-thumper philosophies that were recited when life threw a sneaky curve.

Jackson learned long ago to stop waiting on a gray-haired, bearded, grandfatherly looking man to swoop down from heaven, riding on clouds or in a chariot of fire or a multicolored mother ship from Planet X. Jackson had long dispelled the idea of God, and he'd punched that Jiminy Cricket fella straight in the mouth, silencing the cricket's attempts to be the voice of his conscious. The voice of reason or despair depended on the listener's state of mind. When life was wonderful, when people have a roof over their heads and clothes on their backs, and their bellies were full—that was when men felt blessed, and the voices in their heads told them what was right and wrong. They decided, because of the good lives they were living, that the voice must be the voice of God. But when life threw them that curve, the one they swung at and missed, they'd swing and miss again, striking out on the third. When life left them with no joy, no forward movement, and when all the possessions they had were as empty and intangible as the air between a swing of a bat and a missed ball, then that voice got bad and said life was not worth living. The voice that they praised for giving them such good advice transformed, as they had in their own despondencies, into a gruesome, disfigured, and tormented creature, a voice they came to believe was God's adversary, who now had their ears because of something they'd done or didn't do. *The inner voice of God or the devil? Yeah, right.* Jackson scoffed at the memory of anyone who'd tried to explain to him that God spoke to him in times of need, and the devil spoke in moments of doubt.

The only voice telling Jackson what to do as his own, and he'd be dammed to whatever hell there was before he'd hand over power to God or the devil to make the decisions in his life. Neither would he blame either foundation; the good or the evil couldn't take credit for his accomplishments.

When he heard Sissy speak those words, for the first time, Jackson supposed—and he was sure his assumption was correct—that his sister had actually spoken her true feelings. *Praise God,* Jackson thought, mimicking the ending words to whatever monologue Christians spouted concerning every possible topic there was to be discussed.

"Well, hurry on up, and get him patched together. It ain't safe to be lounging around his house after we done knocked him on his head—not with the cops still looking for Shelly and that missing pastor," Jackson said as he returned to pacing and looking out windows.

"Where we going to go with him?" Sissy asked, a little confused and taken back by this detour from their plan. Their objective had only included confronting Leroy, and using a little muscle if necessary, in order to extract from him the whereabouts of Shelly. Busting Leroy on his noggin to where he was near death, and now learning they were taking him from his home to some other location, caused Sissy's anxiety and swooning sensation to return.

"I know a place. Don't worry. You just get him all mummed up and prepared for a little ride," Jackson said. With that last remark, he went about his sentinel duties as if nothing else was to be asked or said concerning his decision.

3.

When sunlight peeked over the eastern horizon, five pages of Andy's pocket-sized notepad have been written in from top to bottom. He'd been surprised at how open patrons and staff members of Ruby's had been after they'd realized someone else, anyone else was the reason Sunflower county's top law dog came sniffing around the house they occupied. The way to get rid of hounds, those with four legs as well as those with two legs, was to throw them a bone so they could gnaw on it and stop sniffing at the one it had in your pocket. The majority of those he interviewed had much to say about nothing, as most people did when engrossed in conversations having to do with the personal lives of others rather than their own lives. Twenty-three out of the twenty-three potential witnesses he spoke with had something to convey to him when he asked about what they recalled. Andy also asked if anyone had seen Leroy or Shelly after that suspicious night when his wife went missing, and if so, what type of task Leroy or Shelly had been involved in, and if they considered what either had been engaged in seemed normal or out of character.

Andy learned from his few hours interviewing patrons and employees of Ruby's that drunks did not make reliable witness. *That's something we already knew, old' buddy*, the voice of the Detective whispered in his mind. But what he did learn was that for all the time they spent together laughing, drinking, stumbling, and picking one another off of floors, the one other thing the twenty-three shared had been their feelings concerning Leroy Blackman. All of them didn't think much of Andy's only suspect in the case of the missing Shelly Blackman and the recently vanished Reverend Perkins.

The fourth person Andy interviewed was Mrs. Hattie Mae Smith. She'd once been a school teacher, with fifteen years of service at Gentry High School in Inverness. She'd taught freshman through senior year English—or was it social studies? He hadn't been able to recall, and the fact didn't matter. Above everyone he'd spoken with, she provided him with perhaps the best insight concerning the type of relationship Leroy and Shelly Blackman shared.

"She is one of them Seventh-day Adventists—you know, the folks that believe the Lord's Day is Saturday and not Sunday. They got a church near Greenwood, a small building for an organization said to have so much wealth and faith," she commented. Then she continued with her analysis of the Blackmans. "Shelly is a good woman, not much different from the woman I suppose I'd been not too long ago. But like me, she has a weakness for men who need saving, perhaps even more so than me. She looked off into the distance to a place Andy knew was farther than the wall on the other side of the room, beyond the larger world outside of the wood and concrete that had been used to construct Ruby's. The past was a long stretch of miles, lonely and isolated roads that, when travelled down for too long or far enough for a person lose herself in the twisting network of mazelike paths, could only lead her farther toward the center, to where the beast that had spun the trap was waiting to consume her from the inside out. Andy could see in the eyes of Hattie Mae Smith, past her dull, hazed, drunken stare, to the current mess of things caused by misguided decisions. He could see that she was aware that if for not venturing down one wrong path, her life may have consisted of more than waking simply to chase another drunken high and using alcohol as a means to fend off the memories of the past that haunted her in moments of sobriety, like angry ghosts condemned to haunt the places they loathed or loved in life. Hattie Mae Smith walked down that road to the past each and every day of her life, and the only way she was not consumed by the memories was by drinking, consuming enough booze so that she was numbed to thinking of the past, present, or future.

"Shelly being a Seventh-day Adventist, a Christian woman, feels a need to save folks. And what better folk to save then a man who was near to losing his soul? Pulling a man like that from the grip of Satan will make a woman like Shelly Blackman feel she has a purpose." Hattie paused and looked off into that distant place again. She took a sip of whisky from a shot glass that she'd brought with her to the table where Andy was conducting interviews. The whisky seemed to restore her courage, and she continued. "But, Sheriff, you think a man like Leroy Blackman will or can appreciate a woman like Shelly, a woman who only wants to take care of him, to give him a hand so he can lift himself out of the pits of despair." Hattie takes a gulp from the shot glass finishing the remaining drops of whisky. "Of course, a man like Leroy Blackman can't appreciate a good woman. He don't know how the only thing he knows to do is take and take, until there isn't anything left of a good woman except memories of what she'd dreamed of being. Soon, even those embers of hope will fade and burn out from being suffocated by a man like Leroy Blackman."

Hattie looked down at her empty shot glass. The liquid courage within it had all been as consumed as she herself was from the effort of telling the story of women like herself and Shelly Blackman. "Well, Sheriff, there ain't nothing else I have to say about Leroy Blackman. But I guess you weren't looking for no philosophical definition to those questions you asking, are you?"

Andy didn't respond and simply sat there, allowing Hattie to find her way from the maze of memories to a place where she didn't have to suffer in each of her waking thoughts.

"I'll leave you with this, what I believe you really want to know. Do I believe Leroy Blackman could have murdered his wife? Well, you'd better believe I sure as hell do. I believe it as much as I do that tomorrow and the day after that, I'll be sitting here in Ruby's, tossing back whisky shots, and getting drunker than a skunk so that I don't have to remember no more about the demons of my past." Then she pushed the wooden chair she'd been sitting in away from the table, rose to her feet, and strolled across the room to the bar, where she quickly ordered another shot of whisky.

Leroy learned in his final two interviews—his fifteen minutes with Stu Reedman, and the nervous five minutes with Big Lou—less about the emotional inner workings of a man like Leroy Blackman and more of the concrete facts he needed in order to bring him closer to identifying the events leading to the disappearance of Shelly Blackman. "I don't know about what the man did weeks ago. Hell, I can't recall what I did minutes ago," Stu Reedman said. Andy supposed it was a joke or a way to lighten the serious tone of the moment. Andy hadn't been entertained, and he locked eyes with Stu Reedman like a boxer did when facing a challenger. Stu cleared the dryness in his windpipe with a cough and swallow, and then he continued in a more serious tone. "Well, I did see him the next day, driving through Mr. Bean's cotton plantation. You know those dirt paths that kids and moonshiners use when they want to stay hidden from cops when moving their product?" Stu straightened and stopped speaking, as if he'd suddenly remembered to whom he'd been telling secrets. He'd gotten too comfortable, speaking with a cop in a place he felt like himself. "I mean, I've heard moonshiners take those roads, but I can't be sure of that. It's just rumors," he corrected.

Andy waved his hand to dismiss Stu's confession, his gesture ensuring Stu he had no intention (at least not right now) in taking a posse of cops to wait near the roads leading into and out of Mr. Bean's cotton field. He saw the wheels turning inside the mind of Stu Reedman; thankfully, it wasn't a long turn before the circle had been completed.

"Well, Sheriff, I saw him driving along the back roads, the dirt roads intersecting with larger paved roads. Leroy took a turn down a path that leads toward Greenville." Stu paused as if his statement should have been enough for Andy to follow a straight line leading to the questions in his mind. It didn't, so Stu cleared his pipes once again and attempted to make his statement a bit clearer. "Leroy's got folks in Greenville. He's got an uncle with a place deep in the country. I'd say the nearest neighbor is more than five miles away. That'd be his uncle, Richard. Richard's been living out in that country home for near twenty years; everybody says he should sell that land on account of his age and the fact he can no longer keep that structure from falling apart. In fact, Richard's been staying with his brother in Vicksburg since the start of the month—that was when he fell off his roof and broke his hip."

Stu paused, staring at Andy to see if any light bulb popped up over his head. He did not see one, so he continued. "The other reason folks say old Richard, along with anyone else living in that part of the Delta, ought to relocate is because of the Mississippi that flows only a few feet from their backyards. Their homes get flooded two or three times a year, every time after a heavy downpour." Stu paused again, and this time he saw a flicker above Andy's head. "Yeah, Sheriff. I heard it said many folks take things down to that river junk that they want to dispose of. I suppose if you drop something in that part of the Mississippi, it won't ever be found." Stu Reedman provided Andy a place to start looking.

Big Lou had given him a motive for what he believed to be the real reason for Shelly Blackman's disappearance. "He was asking me about some Creole girl, a light-skinned young girl he says was here that night he came here, after his wife went missing."

For a big fella, Lou seemed small when speaking to an officer of the law, as if the sight of a lawman somehow drained his resolve and shrunk him in size. Andy wondered what happened to Big Lou while he'd been in the custody, but he didn't allow the curiosity to linger. He listened as Big Louie finished his answers to the informal interrogation that Andy had just conducted.

"I told him I don't remember no Creole girl, and that seemed to make him really mad, like he thought about taking a swing at me or something. He left this morning not more than ten to fifteen minutes after you arrived, looking happy as a boy with a new bike or something."

Andy stood to make his exit that was when Big Louie dropped his bombshell, almost like he'd scripted the moment so he'd be able to get the desired effect and receive the applause or shock from his audience. "Right when Leroy drove off, I saw Jackson Cousins in that old gray pickup pull out behind him. I noticed that pickup parked in the same spot for a long time. I suppose it had been there since Leroy rolled up in his Olds."

"Jackson Cousins?" Andy said, not being able to place a face with the name.

"Yeah. He's Shelly and Sissy's half-brother. Their father was what you might call a rolling stone type. Shelly and Sissy got a few half siblings on account of their daddy spending many nights away from home." Big Lou suddenly realized Andy had lived most of his life away from the Delta cites; he wouldn't know all the gossip of who did what to whom, and who was related. "Sissy practically raised Jackson. She tried to force-feed him the words of God and turn him into a good man, but I suppose Jackson got a devil in him. I thought I was a tough kid, running the streets, robbing folk, and getting into all sorts of trouble. But I realized when I started hanging with Jackson Cousins that my bad didn't amount to a hill of beans."

Andy grabbed Big Louie by his arm, and when he did, he quickly came to the conclusion that he couldn't move this mountain if he used all of the strength in his body. However, he didn't show Leroy any sign of trepidation. "You saying this Jackson Cousins, a man you admit is bad news, basically staked out Leroy? And when Leroy drove off, Jackson followed him?"

Big Lou nodded to show his agreement with the facts of the story he'd told, and Andy's summation of it. "When he drove off—and this part I can't be sure of—but when Jackson drove off behind Leroy, I could have sore I saw Sissy Cousins, all three hundred pounds of her, squished up in the passenger seat. But I ain't sure it was Sissy, on account I haven't seen her in a long time. The woman in Jackson's passenger seat could have been some other thick-boned women."

Big Lou finished telling his story—a tale Andy felt he could have started with. Andy is having trouble believing someone could be so dimwitted that he couldn't think to tell the most obvious and important part of a story first. Andy tugged on Big Louie's bicep, and Big Louie moved like an elephant on a chain: not because he'd been forced to, but from a trained reaction to follow when being led.

"You are coming with me," Andy ordered.

The demand caused Big Lou to halt in his tracks. "What? Why I got to?" Big Lou tried to think of a hundred excuses for why he couldn't go with Andy, but his mind couldn't get past the confusion to say one aloud.

"You can recognize Jackson's pickup. More important, you know what he looks like. I don't know either, so you're coming with me." Andy pulled on Big Lou's bicep and felt no resistance. "Let's go." They hurried to his Jeep Cherokee.

4.

The coughing and spitting sounds from Jackson's pickup reminded Sissy of old men with diseased lungs from their many years of smoking. Sissy was thankful the sound of an engine on its last leg drowned out another noise, one she believed would disturb her even more if she had to listen to it. She knew Leroy's unconscious body, lying unrestrained in the bed of Jackson's pickup, was bouncing from one side of the truck bed to the other. Sissy had no desire to listen to Leroy's body crash against the hard surface of Jackson's pickup. She wanted Leroy to suffer, especially if he'd done to Shelly what she suspected he had, but she was no sadist. *Not yet, but give it time, Sissy. Keep going down this path, and you'll be a sadist soon—and a masochist too.*

Sissy attempted to ignore the inner voices, along with the images of Leroy's body slamming around. She also did what she could to displace her own character, the Sissy she was accustomed to, from the women who was riding shotgun with her younger brother, like some sibling version of Bonnie and Clyde. *I'm only taking up with Jackson so I can get to the bottom of what has happened to Shelly,* she told herself, trying best she can to believe her words.

Jackson seemed comfortable—at home, one might say. Sissy observed her younger half-brother's behavior: his constant peeks into the rearview mirror, along with the Smith and Wesson he'd tucked between his inner thighs likes he was a mother hen nesting. The danger would and should frighten most people to the point where they'd freeze up like a deer caught in the headlights of a car or truck. The danger seemed to only excite Jackson. Sissy had a sudden and frightening epiphany. *Jackson isn't afraid of being caught. In fact, he may even desire a confrontation with cops so he can test his weapon in a real-life gun fight, a shootout between the men in white hats and those wearing the black ones. Jackson may want to test himself to see if he can do one better than the cowboys who attempted to take down Wyatt Earp and his brothers at the OK Corral. As the bad guy, he wants to be the last man standing*

Sissy looked away from her brother and out the widow, into the landscape that hadn't changed since before the Civil War. The South, especially Mississippi, held to its traditions for good or bad, like a drowning man straining to keep hold of a log, because remaining buoyant was the only thing that mattered, and anyone who thought any different could go straight to hell. Sissy stared into the cotton fields and bottom lands that were mostly a mixture of dry, red soil and swamplands. The seamless, identical miles of land to an outsider may seem no different in one location than another, but Sissy knew the delta like she knew the back of her hand, which was why she was taken aback from her inability to recognize where they were now. The last piece of landscape she'd been familiar with had been a few miles outside of Yazoo City, which was twenty or so miles from where they'd started their journey.

When she'd asked where he was going to take Leroy, Jackson had said not to worry, because he knew a place. Sissy wasn't surprised that her brother had a secret hideaway; it seemed normal for those who lived lives filled with activities causing them to stay one foot ahead of law enforcement. Men like her brother always seemed to know a place, some isolated location far from peering eyes, where they could wait out the heat of whatever crime they'd been involved in to cool.

Sissy closed her eyes. She could have fought a basic need to sleep, but not this feeling, not the exhaustion where the body was extended beyond its natural abilities. The exhaustion was hypnotic, and if she continued focusing on the fatigue, she'd succumb to the rhythm of its spell.

A hypnotizing voice comes in the form of a low, humming roar, a sound like the buzzing emitting from an undisturbed hive of workers, buzzing about and singing in a cadence like men on a chain gang as they worked in unison, their harmonizing tune bringing both peace of mind and a steady, calming sound that lessened the taxing labor of their chores. Sissy fell into a hypnotic rhythm with the sound of rubber tires rolling over gravel dirt and paved roads. She let her shoulders relax, and she'd not noticed she had clinched her jaw so tightly that the tension had been discernible, similar to pulsating jaw muscles when someone ground her teeth and the aftershock vibrated with such intensity that the muscles beneath the jaw moved like the fault lines beneath the crust of the earth.

Sissy's tired eyes played a game of peek-a- boo, shielding themselves behind long black lashes and then exposing themselves again. The game lasted for several minutes before finally her brown eyes tired in efforts to open and closed.

5.

Sissy drowsily woke from her trancelike sleep. Surprisingly, she was not rested but, she had a feeling Sissy supposed bears felt when they first rose from the bewitching effects of hibernation. She was a bit confused and weighed with the burden of loss.

"We're here," Jackson unceremoniously announced.

Could have guessed that much on my own, Sissy thought, annoyed by Jackson's truculent mood swings. One minute he reminded her of the misbehaving youth she'd been unable to wrangle in. His other mood was just as antagonistic as his childlike combativeness that she feared as much as she loathed. It was the personality of a bully that lifted Jackson to tops of mountains, a warrior like temperament a psyche that allowed for him to reign as the king of soulless and morally bankrupt people residing in the valley beneath his snowy or rocky hilltop.

"Where is here?" Sissy asked as she surveyed the landscape through lenses still fogged by the thin layer of mucus that often covered the eyes when one first woke. "I don't know this area. Where are we? Are we far from Yazoo City?"

"You ain't supposed to know about this place. Ain't nobody supposed to know? That's the whole point," Jackson said in that truculent way that Sissy despised. The voice said, "Fuck you." Though in Sissy's mind, she didn't say that foul word. She said "Fudge you" but the phrase carried the same meaning, as if she'd said the bad word.

Sissy looked around, and all she could see was what may have at one point been a soy bean or cotton plantation. Either due to a farmer losing his land from an inability to pay what he owed to the government, or perhaps due to the soil turning bad due to overplanting, the ground became impossible, and the farmer had moved on to another plantation or vocation.

"Over there. That's where we taking him," Jackson said as he pointed one of his long, thin digits toward a spot that looked just as void of civilization as the remaining landscape, overgrown in weeds and grass. Jackson smiled, and Sissy was surprised to see in his physical manifestation of inner joy, Jackson's grin had the same delish expression that it'd had when he'd been a boy, when he'd attempted to use his charm to conceal thoughts of his true motives, which in his childhood proved to be mischievous rather than good intentions. *He hasn't changed, not one bit. And he never will,* Sissy thought.

"I guess in this here area, if goes as far back as slave days," Jackson began as he walked around to the bed of his pickup, where he removed the tarp covering Leroy and some of his own personal items. The majority of the tools were for his criminal vocation, equipment he used to break and enter into homes or business: ropes, metal pipes, glass cutters, and so on.

"On this piece of land, there'd once been a big ole plantation home. There ain't no record of its existence or anything, but I know it was here on account of what I've discovered." Jackson poked Leroy in his ribs, nudging him with the barrel of his Colt .45 hard enough so that even if Leroy was pretending to be unconscious, the pain of being poked in his ribs wouldn't allow him to stay quiet.

Leroy moaned and mumbled a few incoherent phrases: something about a mule, and a name—Lorna or Lana. Jackson couldn't make out which name, but it sounded like one of those two. "Must have been one of those grand, palatial plantation homes." *Palatial* was another dictionary word Jackson had learned during his time behind bars. "The kind of mansion you see in the old movies, where white folks sit in swings on large porches, drinking lemonade while discussing how they'll profit from the labor of slaves so the owners can continue sitting and drinking lemonade until they are old, fat, and useless." Jackson tugged on the rope knots tied around Leroy's wrists and ankles. "There ain't nothing left of that grand mansion that can be seen if you're standing here and looking out into the fields of weeds and barren land." He strolled around to the back of his pickup and unlocked the bolts, freeing the tailgate. The hatchbacks fell flat, allowing Jackson to easily climb into the cargo area of his Chevy.

He stood tall over the weeded ground among his chainsaws, crowbars, glasscutters, ropes, and Leroy's body. "Over there, Sissy, buried beneath what may be a near a hundred years of new earth, weeds, and who knows what else," Jackson said, using his long, thin digit once again to reference the location of which he was speaking. "What remains of that palatial home, the only part of it I suppose that could have endured years of weathering harsh elements, along with man's need to bulldoze or use a wrecking ball to topple, is that one part of a place that can remain hidden away from man's eyes, along with having the sort of solid foundation to not succumb to natural, deteriorating factors caused by the time and conditions."

Listening to Jackson speak caused Sissy to realize that if her half brother, a young man she'd attempted to raise and show a better way of life, applied himself to more than the devil's work, he had the sort of mind that could lift in above his destructive beginnings.

Jackson abruptly kicked Leroy in his side with a booted foot. When Leroy moaned in pain and again began murmuring those incoherent phrases, Jackson's smile reappeared. Sissy rethought her Jackson's ability to rise above the lot in life into which he'd been born. *He is full of sin, full of evil. He'll never change,* she reminded herself so as to not forget the sort of person her half-brother was.

When Jackson grabbed Leroy by his ankles and dragged him across the metal surface of his pickup, forcefully jerking the bound body from time to time in order to pull it over tools that halted progression, Sissy cringed from the pain she knew Leroy must feel. She didn't really have any sympathy for Leroy, no more than someone may have for a killed wolf that would have ripped out someone's jugular vein with sharp canines. Watching any living thing suffer, be it innocent or vile, wasn't easy to witness—unless it was someone like her half-brother. She believed he may enjoy viewing such a horrible thing as a creature taking its final breath. Sissy cringed once again when Leroy's body reached the edge of the hatch, and instead of carefully lowering him to the ground, Jackson allowed the body to fall full force, landing hard on the dry, rocky earth. Jackson continued providing Sissy with his historical version of events that he believed led to the demise of a great Southern palatial home, and how he alone had benefited from something of that home having survived in an immortal fashion, perhaps as the pyramids of Egypt were thought to have done.

"Beneath the ground, protected from winds, rain, and whatever nature has to offer, and away from the prying and wanting eyes of men, a portion of that palatial home has endured."

Suddenly, as if a light switch had been flicked on in her brain, allowing her to not only see but understand with more clarity, Sissy understood what Jackson had so cryptically been explaining. Beneath the ground where once stood a grand Southern home was the mansion's cellar. *Jackson's personal dwelling beneath the earth, his own residence close to the hell in which he will spend eternity,* Sissy thought.

You'll be spending time in hell's fires with him, if you go down into that basement, the voice of God said in her head.

Jackson dragged Leroy by his ankles, the slow progression of kidnapper and his prisoner followed by Sissy. All three were travelling about one hundred feet over rocky, hard earth and through prickly grass and yellow weeds. When they reached an area in the middle of what, from a passing glance, appeared unwelcoming to human occupation and as vacant as someone looking out at the surface of the ocean, Sissy could see why someone like Jackson would value the discovery of such a place. *God only knows what he does down there, and what he'll do in order to make Leroy talk. Whatever he does, Sara Cousins, you'll be accountable as well. Accessories of a crime are guilty and are punished alongside those who commit the crime. You'll burn alongside Jackson. Sara Cousins, his sin will become yours.*

Sissy pushed aside the warning voice like a child ignoring a parental message. The parental voice would refer to the person with a full name so that one would not be confused of from whom the warning came. *Sara Cousins, you'll be accountable as well,* the fatherly voice of God said. Her heavenly father had called to her using her birth name, so she'd not be confused as to whose voice was providing her with the warning message. *Sara Cousins, his sin will become yours.*

Jackson used his booted feet to kick away rocks and dirt, and to stomp upon broadleaf signalgrass, yellow nutsedge, and other weeds threatening to reclaim the hidden secret beneath the earth. When he'd cleared the space of debris, Jackson reached down and grabbed hold of a handle. The door led into a cellar that had once been the basement level of a palatial home. He lifted Leroy by his shoulders as if he was no more than a sack of potatoes, maneuvering Leroy's limp body to the opening in the earth. Then he dropped him feet first into the lightless cellar. "Welcome to hell, Leroy," Jackson said. Then he climbed down into the darkness.

He said it. He said welcome to hell. Can't be no denying where you at now, Sara Cousins, if you didn't know it before, If you want to ignore my warnings, if you want to ignore every intuition in your gut telling you to turn tale and run. How you going to ignore the man's own words, his own admission to this being his place, being hell? Somehow, Sissy found the courage—or was it something else? She'd felt the emotion, dismissed it, and placed it away, hadn't she? She believed she had and wouldn't allow herself to consider that anger propelled her forward, causing her to ignore God's voice just as a kid swept aside a parental mantra ingrained in his mind since he'd first been able to understand Mama and Daddy's words. *This is for Shelly, for Reverend Perkins,* Sissy thought as she moved forward, blind to (or in spite of) trepidations caused by her own lifelong lessons of what was right and wrong.

6.

Andy thought about reaching for the microphone connected to his police scanner and calling for backup. Then he withdrew his outstretched hand. Right now, he only had assumptions and vague stories told by local drunks concerning Leroy Blackman. Sure, he could haul a suspect in based on limited evidence of having committed a crime. But usually that circumstantial amount of information didn't hold up in court and wasn't enough to keep a guilty man behind bars where he belonged. Instead of calling for backup he may or may not need, Andy decided to probe a little deeper into the life of Leroy Blackman. What better place to analyze the cogitation behind a man's actions than entering his personal space? The way a man lived and how he organized his personal environment could tell a good detective more about that person's state of mind than speaking with those who believed they knew him or hours spent interrogating him.

God-given talent was the thing that had made Andy one of the top detectives in Atlanta. Cops discussed topics concerning the job, their home lives, and worldly news events, but they also discussed who they believed to be the number one detective in the city. Before years on the job wore at his state of mind like termites chewing on the wooden foundation of a home; before stresses of his career ate away the sturdiness of his resolve, Andy's names passed through the mouths of numerous coworkers when they cast their verbal ballots for who they believed was number one. Narrations of Andy's feats had been passed along in that old way of verbally recording tribal and family historical accounts, where elders committed to memory events that they in turn relayed to others. Elders may or may not accurately retell accounts of ancestral monologues, and so that fiction could become greater than truth, which after many years of telling and retelling was often the case.

Andy's accomplishments, those actual facts of what he did or didn't do, were perhaps fused with some fiction, the adding and taking away of events so that a narrative was not so much a complete fabrication but was relayed with enough guile that the line between fact and fiction was blurred. When the feats of men were told in a mythological manner that was when the actual sweat, labor, guts, and tenacity used in accomplishment was diminished; mere hard work was disregarded; and a man's success was credited to some supernatural ability. The image of the hero was then born, a man or woman who could walk through fire, dodge speeding bullets, or (in Andy's case) uncover clues to clearly see a way leading toward solving a crime, when other cops found themselves stumbling around in the dark without a glimmer of light to lead them in the right direction.

The Detective was not some superpower-endowed hero, but a man who'd spent years of sacrifice honing skills and replacing what other men valued—his wife, his children, a normal existence—in order to be the best at what he did. *Was it worth all the loss, Andy?* a voice asked as the thought entered his mind Andy didn't answer the question; he never did, when that voice of regret queried him. He pushed past the lamentations and moved forward to where he could hear the voice of the Detective, the persona that may have been the reason for his sudden crack and descent from top cop to sheriff of Mayberry. He moved past this annoyance as well, because neither his regret nor his affliction that the insanity may have derived from, following a voice in his head, could help him in finding and arresting the murderer he believed Leroy Blackman had become.

"Sheriff, you really think Leroy done killed his wife and that pastor?" Big Louie asked, snapping Andy from thoughts of his past and the questioning of his own sanity.

"Don't know. Could be." Andy was short in his reply to Big Louie's query, and his behavior had not been accidental. He didn't want to chat it up with Big Louie, not on the subject of the weather, how he thought the Mississippi Valley State football team would fare this season, or whether they'd ever have another player with the skills of Jerry Rice. He especially didn't want to discuss with him his current investigation of Shelly Blackman's and the Reverend Perkins's possible murders. *Just stay in your seat, fella. Look out of the window, sniff the air, and take in huge gulps of it through an open mouth. Wag your tail and be a good boy.* Andy could hear the Detective's laugh inside his mind, discovering humor in what he'd just said. Andy couldn't help but notice a bit of what he thought may be the cackle of a man not quite in his right state of mind. He ignored his feelings and continued on. At this point, there wasn't anything else for him to do. *You're in the shit now, boy, and you're not going like it. But looks like we're going to do some swimming in some foul, repugnant-smelling crap before all is said and done.* Andy kept his focus on the road ahead. They'd arrive at the home of Andy's uncle in less than five minutes—the home Stu Reedman had said often was flooded in rainy seasons due to its close proximity to the Mississippi River, and the riverbank where Stu implied many objects were tossed into and never found.

7.

The hip that Old Man Richard Blackman had broken while attempting to resurface his decaying roof had mended, but from the way he hobbled around, one would not think the fractured bone as strong enough to carry his weight. At any point in his hobbling from one place to another, it looked like that the hip would simply give out.

Mangy mutts varying in size, color, and degrees of patches of flesh revealed in places where the mange ate away fur emerged from beneath crawl spaces under a porch. The coon dogs resembled fire-scratched and ferocious hounds of hell, howling and growling as they circled an unfamiliar vehicle, eager to get at the two men sitting within the metal barricade protecting them from sharp canines.

"Go on, get. Get, ye hear me?" Richard Blackman, Leroy's uncle on his father's side, shooed his dogs away. His hounds obeyed him as if he were Mr. Fire and Brimstone himself.

"Mean dogs," Big Lou whispered more as self-commentary than to garner any return comments from Andy, who big Louie figured out was in no mood for small talk.

The coon dogs tucked their tails at hearing the sound of their master's voice, which also caused them to scurry in quick attempts to flee whatever wrath they'd been conditioned to fear. They returned to the only place where they felt safe, beneath the house in crawl spaces too small for adult men to reach without getting on their hands and knees and snaking their way in. After the dogs went back to their hidden labyrinths, Andy opened his door and stepped out of his Jeep. He looked back to notice Big Lou, frozen in his seat staring into the dark space beneath the porch. *So the giant mountain's kryptonite is a fear of cops and dogs.* Andy and the Detective took notice and placed the information into that file cabinet where useful tidbits were stored.

"Come on, big fella. The dogs not going to come back out, not with Richard keeping them at bay," Andy said.

"Suppose you here on account of that nephew of mine?" said Richard Blackman in a raspy voice not sounding much different from the dry, barking sound made by his coon dogs.

"Yes, sir. I got some information that your nephew may have come by your place around the time his wife went missing," Andy explained. He was amazed by the speed bad news traveled in a small region of towns that moved at a turtle's slow, methodical pace.

"I weren't here. Ain't been home for nearly three months. Been staying with my brother up in Vicksburg, waiting for this bone to set so's I can march again." Richard tapped his right hip with his palm to indicate the obvious, just in case Andy and that big fella easing his way from the passenger side like he wasn't sure the ground would support his bulk were so daft they didn't notice that the dark meat, bone, flesh, and muscle wasn't working well as it had been before he fell from his roof.

"I know, Mr. Blackman," Andy began, but he was cut short before he could conclude his statement.

"My pops, he was Mr. Blackman. I'm simply Richard, or as my friends refer to me, Red." Richard hobbled over to where Andy was standing next to his Jeep Cherokee, and nearer to Big Lou, who was keeping his right hand on the handle of the passenger side door—and both his eyes glued to the crawl space.

The thin-framed but muscular elder man was in good physical condition except for his hobble caused by a recent broken hip and his Chris Cringle beard and hair Red could have passed for a man far younger than his actual age. However, neither the hair on his head nor his chin was long enough for him to pass as Santa Clause. Even a chocolate-colored Santa would have to grow hair atop his head and beneath his chin to a longer length than the thick stubble that grew atop of Richard Blackman's scalp and beneath his long, angular chin.

"Now, before we get started, Sheriff, I'm gonna tell you something, a fact about me and my kin, a piece of information you may or may not wish to believe. Don't mean much of anything to me, either way your mind wants to go with it." Richard moved the long, single strand of hay straw that was clinched between his top and bottom molars from the left to the right side of his mouth, using only his lips to push the hay across his dry dark smoker's lips. When the piece of straw, about the width and length of a pencil, made it from one side of his mouth to the other, Richard filled in Andy about how things were between him and some of his kin.

"People say blood's thicker than water, but I can guarantee anyone saying that round here ain't in no way a Blackman or related to those I share a name with." The pencil-sized straw was pushed to the side of Richards's mouth where it had been at start of his story. "I have a good relationship with one brother, the one in Vicksburg I stayed with while my hip was mending. I have a sister I'm close to, but I don't see much of her anymore, not since she moved to Chicago nearly twenty years ago. Don't blame her for leaving. If I had the mind to get out of the Delta instead of focusing on women and drinking when I'd been twenty years younger, I'd have made that move myself." Richard looked far into the distance of his past. Then he shook his head in that slow, methodical way folks did when they were showing regret. "Well, I'm still here, and those kin that remain here in the Delta, I don't have much care for them. I suppose that's okay, because I figure the feeling is mutual."

Andy listened to Richard's story, doing what he could to suppress the screaming voice of impatience begging him to reach out, grab hold of Richard's shoulders, and shake him until the man stopped beating around the bush and got to the point of his tale. But Andy kept his eagerness to move the conversation along at bay, allowing the elder man to complete his thoughts.

"With that said, all I can say is I ain't got the sort of relationship one might think an uncle should with his brother's kid. Sure, Leroy comes by from time to time, usually to get a part for his vehicle or to share a drink of homemade brew. But other than those visits, we don't spend any time together."

"I understand, Mr. Blackman—I mean Richard," Andy corrected, not wanting to hear another monologue concerning who was the real Mr. Blackman. "During my investigation into Leroy's missing wife, Shelly, I came across some information that led me to believe she, Leroy, or the both of them may have spent some time at your place while you were up in Vicksburg." While Andy spoke, the Detective looked for signs, nonverbal clues similar to what a champion poker player looked for when determining whether his opposition's blank stare provided any indications to the cards he held in his hand. When the Detective didn't notice any odd tells, Andy set aside all beliefs of Richard being an accessory in the disappearance of Shelly Blackman or Reverend Perkins. "I'd like to look around your place on account of acquiring the information about Leroy heading in this direction, if you don't mind."

"Look all you want. Don't matter to me. Like I said, I don't have nothing to say about what Leroy may or may not have done," Richard Blackman said, and with that, he hobbled away from Andy.

8.

The roots of trees were thick as a man's thigh. From a distance, green ashes, conifers, and elms stood, and their roots tunneled through the earth, creating mazes of underground routes in their search for moisture, stretching from between fifteen and twenty feet. Roots went in a direction where the remains what had once been the Southern plantation structure as, a palatial home. They worked deep underground, where only the roots of trees and other burrowing life-forms existed, their activities covered from view by several feet of sediment.

Sissy stood in what had once been a basement, a narrow corridor of space resembling, after years of neglect, more an underground cavern than a lower level of beneath a grand home. Jackson had lit the wicks of several candles he'd placed in tiny spaces throughout the basement, in order to provide light to see. Jackson had provided Leroy with the quickest but more painful route into the underground level. He followed the ground where he'd dropped his prisoner, but his route made less impact. He scaled down a rope ladder he had constructed as a simpler way to make his descent from the opening of the basement to its soil-covered floor. He'd even used some of the thick roots as anchors to support his bulk and tie off the rope. Sissy's descent down the narrow passageway caused her to feel like Alice must have felt when she'd first entered the rabbit hole, not knowing whether she'd reached the bottom.

She'd been thankful for the candlelight when she reached the bottom. If not for the flickering orange and white glow from the wax sticks, she may have panicked from being so far under the earth in such a small space. Remains of the basement, the portion of walls, floors, and rooms that had not been completed, were covered in collapsing rocks and soil. The space was around the size of a modern-day master bedroom, minus the closet. That made the space available extremely small.

"Welcome," Jackson said with a shit-eating grin on his face. "Mi casa es su casa." He stretched his arm out to the side in the direction of a mattress and leather recliner, both littered with dirt. Sissy moved toward the recliner, brushed dirt off of where she'd place her rear, and took a seat, ignoring the squeaking sounds of protest made by the springs beneath the tattered cushion.

Jackson went to work preparing Leroy for his torture, dragging him to one corner, looping the loose rope binding Leroy's arms over a thick root, and then securing it by tying a hangman's knot and extending Leroy's arms over his head. Then he strolled over to a blue water cooler sitting at the edge of the mattress, opened it, and retrieved one plastic container of water, which he tossed toward Sissy. Jackson's toss had been accurate, and the plastic bottle hit her right in the hands. But she fumbled it, and it slipped past her and to the ground. While she bent at the waist to retrieve her dropped container, Jackson removed another, opened it, and gulped down water like racehorse. After he'd finished quenching his thirst, he removed a third container, unscrewed the top, walked back to where he'd secured Leroy, and poured the water over the top of the man's head.

"Wakey, wakey," he whispered as water drenched Leroy, flowing over his face and blood-stained shirt. Leroy moaned as he returned to consciousness.

9.

Piles of junk metal, pieces of wooden furniture in various levels of decay, multiple sizes of rubber car and truck tires, along with numerous other items collected by someone who considered someone else's trash a treasure littered Richard Blackman's yard. Andy decided he'd allow Big Louie to plod his way through the mountain of junk. Partly it was because he didn't think finding a clue within the junkyard would be easy. Also, he'd be able to do his searching on his own. He chose to search along the edges of the Mississippi, which traveled behind Richard's backyard, hoping the land not as littered in human trash would reveal something to lead him to learning something more about the missing Shelly Blackman or Reverend Perkins. He peeked over his left shoulder in the direction he'd left his reluctant deputy to notice Big Louie was peering into the space beneath the porch, where the coon dogs had scattered; then the big man briefly eyed the ground for any clues of the missing.

Andy had almost decided to call it quitting time and move on to the next line of to-dos in his mental rolodex when he saw it. About ten feet from where Richard's backyard dropped into the Mississippi, wedged between a branch and stump-sized stone, he saw a women's shoe. When he got closer, he knew from the small size that the shoe was indeed the size a woman or child would wear. He picked it up by its black laces. *A women's loafer,* the Detective answered for him. Andy wondered what size the loafer was, and he also wondered what sized shoe Shelly Blackman wore. Further, he wondered where the matching shoe might be, and if the red-stained color he recognized as blood would match the blood type of Shelly Blackman.

10.

The baptism Jackson had given Leroy woke him from a sleep that was much like the darkness sinners discovered themselves within before cleansing water and acknowledgment of their evil ways provided an expunging of their unholy deeds. *Time to pay the devil his due,* Sissy Cousins thought, and she watched with anticipation as the fog of unconsciousness released its grasp on Leroy.

When Leroy regained consciousness, the first thing he thought was that he'd died in his sleep and had awakened in hell. The damp, small space with ominous roots reaching out for him appeared like deformed appendages of some demonic beast. Flickering lights of candles leaped from darkness to inflict pain on his flesh for an eternity of burning without hope of redemption.

But then he heard a familiar voice—one that assured him he'd not died or fallen into the devil's pit of fire and brimstone. "What you have done with my sister, Leroy Blackman? You tell me now, or I swear before God I can't be responsible for what pains you'll suffer."

Leroy cocked his head toward the sound of that familiar voice, looking like a confused cocker spaniel when his owner spoke in more than the few human phrases he understood. "Sissy? Sissy Cousins, that you?" Leroy asked in the confused, slurred voice of someone suddenly realizing a truth of circumstances after a night of overconsumption of moonshine. Leroy hadn't yet figured out where he was or how he gotten to this place, but he had knew one thing was for certain: if the Bible thumper Sissy Cousins was here with him, then he wasn't in hell."

Or are ya, Chocolate? Wouldn't that be a sort f hell, having to live an eternity looking at and listening to Sissy Cousins? Lana Monroe said. He looked around within the dim cave but couldn't find Lana's face. He suddenly got angry because if this was it, if death had swooped down using his long, sharp, concaved blade to reap rewards of his harvest, then he'd taken Leroy prematurely, before he'd had a chance to claim his promised fame and fortune.

"Moody! Mr. Moody Johnson!" Leroy screamed in a demanding voice, his fear of Mr. Moody abated. If he was dead and in hell, then what did it matter in what tone he spoke to someone as powerful and evil as he believed Moody Johnson was?

The voice that answered his call hadn't been that of Moody Johnson or even Sissy Cousins. "You'd better focus Leroy. Focus on here and now, and answer what my sister done asked you. Then we gonna talk about your Mr. Moody Johnson."

11.

Discovery of one blood-stained shoe wasn't enough to call in the cavalry in full force to one location. Otherwise, Andy might discover he had overreached based on limited information, causing him, along with his deeds, to be remembered in history in a more infamous than glorifying manner. Although neither Andy nor his alter ego believed a woman's shoe should be discovered in the backyard of Leroy Blackman's uncle, ten feet from where the Mississippi River claimed ownership of space from the land, they didn't wish to risk it being tossed in with Monday morning trash collected by city garbage trucks and hauled away to vast trash sites, where the overabundance of humankind's purchases were stored.

He'd contacted two patrol cars, one to intercept Leroy at his home, and one collect information concerning Jackson's and Sissy Cousins' suspicious behavior.

Andy stayed on the main road on his return drive from Richard Blackman's home, heading to where Leroy lived. He knew a man on the run wouldn't make his getaway—if that was what Leroy was planning—by sticking to the most obvious exit out of the area. He also believed if what he'd heard of Jackson Cousins, a man with an evil streak as long and dreadful as the highway took on his way to hell, was true, then Leroy wouldn't survive.

"You'll recognize Jackson's vehicle and Jackson, if you spot either?" Andy asked Big Lou, shouting over the roar of his Jeep Cherokee's engine and the cool, afternoon breeze that came through the open windows.

"Yes, sir," Big Lou responded, although he silently hoped he'd be spared of encountering them.

Should have headed to Leroy's right after leaving Ruby's. Might have headed off either Jackson Cousins or Leroy Blackman before they met up, if that's what's happened, the Detective said.

Andy responded to the Detective's questioning of his motives and decisions. *If I didn't go to Richard's house first, I wouldn't have discovered the shoe. With all the dogs and it being on a slope leading to the river's edge, there isn't any telling if it would've remained where it was a day from now.*

Well, guess it don't matter now. What's done is done. We still have a dog in this race. The lead hounds ain't too far ahead, the Detective concluded.

Yeah, I agree, Andy thought, and he placed pressure on the gas pedal, increasing the speed

12.

When Mr. Smith and Mr. Wesson had developed their Colt .45, they hadn't had in mind for it to be used like a mere stone. They'd created the weapon to be a more modern, effective way to subdue and, if necessary, take a life. But humans reverted to their primitive nature, their basic instincts, and no matter the advances in technology, some things could be removed or replaced by easier, more effective ways of accomplishing a task.

Jackson raised his weapon, pulled his arm back like his a pitcher ready to throw a fastball over, and he let loose, striking Leroy on his right cheek with the butt of his gun. "Where in hell is Shelly, boy? I can go at this all night long. How long you think you going to last?"

Leroy attempted to roll with the punch that had been amplified by the hard surface of the Colt .45, but a concrete wall prevented him from being able to maneuver his head enough to angle it away from the incoming blow. The pistol whipping felt like being pummeled by a man using brass knuckles, or at least Leroy thought it may feel the same. He wasn't sure because he had never been struck by someone who'd used brass knuckles over their bone, and this was the first time he'd been pistol whipped. But he was sure there were only slight variations in level of pain and damage inflicted by either.

Leroy moved his tongue across the inside of his right cheek, searching for damage. He was also able to move a section of bone on the underside of his jaw, and he was sure this time the blow had broken or fractured the bone.

Chocolate, ye done got yourself in a mess. This one is mighty mean. I think he likes inflicting a bit of pain on you. Leroy knew Lana was right about Jackson. Leroy hardly knew Shelly's younger brother, but what knowledge he did have, he'd learned from tales of Jackson's exploits. The boy had a bit of sadomasochist in him. In truth, both of those traits were oozing from Jackson's genetics, and it was the dominant part of his personality. Lana was right: Jackson was getting off on inflicting pain. His pecker was probably stiffer than a kid after having a glancing view of white cotton fabric underneath a girl's skirt as she crossed her legs.

He noticed in his peripheral vision flickering candlelight, or a shadow cast within the dimly lit room, or a combination of both. Leroy rolled his head in the direction of the movement of light, or some shadow. Lana Monroe was standing clear as day in a corner opposite of where he was hanging by his wrists and is being pistol whipped. Her exotic green orbs followed his stare, and he was confused by the lack of attention given to her presence. Then he recalled what had happened when he'd reached out to touch her, and what his mama had said: *Leroy, you know you're completely insane.* Now, here in the dark, he supposed what his mama had said may in fact be true. Either Lana was a ghost or, worse, she simply didn't exist except in his mind.

Lana followed Leroy's eyes to where they'd been led to because of a flicker or shadow in his sight line.

"Wow, she's a huge one, ain't she?" Lana said when laying eyes on Sissy Cousins sitting in an old, worn leather recliner that almost wasn't wide enough to contain her girth. Leroy had heard Shelly's voice, but thoughts of her had disappeared from his mind when Jackson began his pistol whipping.

"One doughnut away from the few pounds that will advance her from the three hundreds into the four-hundred-pound club," Leroy said, but his words were choked off by a mouth full of blood and saliva.

"What? What you say?" Jackson demanded, leaning in close to Leroy's face in order to get a better vantage point to hear and understand the muffled words. Leroy spat a mouth full of blood and saliva into the face of Jackson. The man didn't budge or have a look of revulsion on his face. He didn't even wipe the blood away. He simply smiled through his blood-stained face. "That's one for you, Leroy. Now here's one from me." *Crack!* Leroy didn't have to move his tongue across the inside of his jaw that time; he knew as the pain surged from his jaw to his head, and it seemed to his entire body, that the strike had broken his jaw for sure.

"Ouch. That one gonna leave a mark, for sure," Lana replied. The sound of her voice was the only thing preventing him from passing out from the pain.

When Leroy spat again, losing three teeth three teeth went with the blood and saliva.

"I think you need to tell what they want to know, Chocolate. A few more of those, and you may be eating your diner from a needle in your arm, and the only thoughts you'll be able to formulate will be the same as those logical deductions made by a piece of squash."

Leroy began laughing and spitting up blood and more fragments of his busted teeth. He caught a glimpse of Jackson's arm cock back, but before the man could release another hit, Leroy gurgled out, "I'll take you to where she is, to where Reverend Perkins is."

"Yeah, that's right. It's about time we introduce Jackson and Sumo over there to our friend Mr. Moody Johnson. Then we will see who get the last laugh," Lana whispered. Jackson nodded his head in agreement.

The End of the Beginning

Me and the Devil Walking Side by Side.

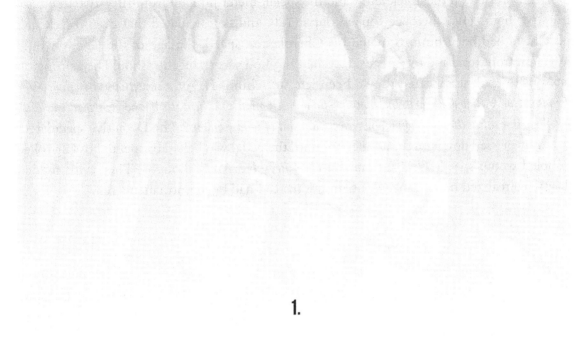

1.

THE ACTUAL SIGHT of it was like looking directly into the sun in its fullness: it struck one with such force that one had to look away and then look again from another angle, so one would be able to focus enough to make out details missed by a sudden flash that blurred the vision.

"That's him," Big Lou yelled as he looked back over his shoulder through the rear window of Andy's Jeep, focusing his eyes on the speeding pickup barreling down the road they'd just come from, speeding in a westerly direction along Highway 9.

Andy spun the steering column of his Jeep Cherokee until the vehicle made an about-face. He hadn't had to use skills learned in fast-pace pursuit of criminals in the years since he'd left the force in Atlanta, but fortunately muscle memory took over, and the unexpected turn didn't catch him off balance; he quickly brought the vehicle under control. From the time Big Lou had turned and recognized Jackson's pickup to when Andy had made his turn, Jackson had travelled ten miles from the spot.

"He must have seen us. He had to have. We would have gained ground on him if he was driving at a normal speed," Big Lou said.

Andy didn't respond to the commentary. Of course he'd seen them. The majority of folks, especially those with a criminal mindset, recognized Andy's black Jeep Cherokee. If they weren't sure the Jeep belonged to him, the bold black Sheriff Department of Sunflower County insignia on both sides of his doors was a dead giveaway.

Andy pressed on the accelerator, and the speedometer jumped from fifty-five to eighty miles per hour. His Cherokee topped out at 120, and he calculated that even if Jackson's old Chevy had been built to match his Cherokee in speed, the age of the Chevy would prevent it from reaching top speeds. But then Big Lou was right: they should be gaining on Jackson. Instead, it appeared they'd been left far behind. *He got a supercharged engine? One of those vehicles that don't look like nothing from observation, but beneath the hood, where you can't see, there is a shiny chrome engine powered by a heard of wild stallions?* The Detective speculated.

Andy pressed down on the accelerator until the pedal was halted by metal. His Cherokee wobbled to top speed. *How fast can that old Chevy be?* Andy thought. Then with sudden clarity, he realized he's not been outrun but instead had been outmaneuvered.

2.

Fudge rockets and fiddlesticks. I'll be a witch's wart, Sissy thought when she first noticed the sheriff's vehicle making its way toward them on the eastbound side of the road. Jackson's reaction to seeing the sheriff's vehicle triggered his flight instincts, causing him to stomp his foot on the accelerator of his Chevy as if he meant to kick the gas pedal through the metal floorboard. Sissy's next thought on account of Jackson's reaction entered her mind at the exact moment Jackson's booted foot provided his Chevy with a kick similar to one man placing a boot on another man's rear when he needed him to move quickly. Sissy's thought had been that her half-brother was a cotton-headed ninny-mugger, and that she'd never known anyone more able to fit a polite description. Sissy wrapped her chubby fingers around the seat belt, which had only barely provided enough slack as she'd stretched it around her midsection. Most cars' seat belts fit so snug around her belly that when she removed them later when she was in the bath or changing into her sleeping attire, she'd notice red blotching marks indicial in width of the seat belt imprinted on her stomach.

Sitting in the passenger seat of Jackson's Chevy and strapped in at her waist next to the cotton-headed ninny-mugger behind the wheel and another fool hog-tied and concealed from view by a brown tarp, and now with a sheriff hot on their heels, Sissy felt like a chocolate teapot for allowing herself to be in such a perilous situation. Only a totally incapable person, a chocolate teapot, would allow herself to have been led on a ride with a posted warning sign stating this ride could be dangerous to her health and life. She'd ignored the danger and stood in line, and when the ride started, she sat her rear down in a front-row seat. She'd been blind to the mistake she'd made until shed reached the summit of an uphill climb and looked over to see how high her stupidity had taken her. *Only a chocolate teapot would allow herself to take a seat in a chair on a ride she knew could end her life,* Sissy thought.

The road was one that could have been mistaken for nothing more than a small pathway. It was overrun with wild vegetation, and from the condition, one would think it was not clear enough to be traversed by even bipedal commuters. It was hardly the sort of road that a vehicle of any size would be able to make its way along. But that had to be the answer, the solution to the puzzle of why he'd not run down Jackson's pickup. Andy spun the steering wheel once again, slowing as much as needed so he'd not place too much stress on one side of his Jeep, causing it to become unbalanced and flip over.

Night was approaching, and with the coming evening hours, darkness would follow. Most people had no idea how dark the world could be when the sun set. There was a blackness in the night, as well in the hearts of men that was all consuming. That darkness, if allowed to spread, would move across the land, feasting on light within humankind like swarms of locusts that formed a dark cloud of organic life, moving as one giant beast toward fields and devouring everything green. Andy couldn't explain why neither the usual perspective of the Detective nor his inner voice of reason and clarity provided him with answers. He could not dismiss an eerie feeling, one urging him to keep moving. *Don't lose Jackson Cousins.* Because if he does, then there would be more killing before the night came to an end.

3.

Jackson's pickup plowed through rows of yellow nutsedge signalgrass and sida broadleaf, among other plant life. There was such an abundance of weeds and bushes that they had constructed an almost impenetrable wall sturdy enough that not even a motorized vehicle could plow its way through.

"Damn it!" Jackson yelled as he slammed his fist on the steering column. He only needed to make it another four or five miles through the overrun road, and then they'd be in Yazoo City. Then it was just another mile or so, if Leroy wasn't lying to him about where he'd left Shelly and the reverend.

"Get out. We're hoofing it from here on," Jackson said, opening his driver's side door. Fifteen, twenty minutes—that's how long it would have taken them to drive into Yazoo City's town limits. Hoofing it—especially moving with the dead weight he'd be caring in the form of Leroy, and Sissy's laboring efforts—would mean they'd move at a snail's pace. *Cops done probably figured out you taken this road by now. They'll be closing in on you soon, and with these two in tow, they'll catch you,* Jackson told himself.

"How far we have to walk until we get there?" Heavy, raspy, breathing followed each word that exited Sissy's mouth. She hadn't even taken one step and already sounded like she was walking a few miles uphill.

Gonna have to ditch her soon. No way will she keep up. And if you slow down to her inchworm speed, the cops will catch up for sure. Leave her now, Jackson thought. He stopped in order to consider what his plan was if he was caught. He wouldn't have very many options. He could lower his head and make a dash for it, but there were always too many cops, too many legs and lungs for him to outrun. Running wasn't a go, but his second option wouldn't provide him much more success—unless one counted the highlights of his encounter with the cops told in print and on the six and ten o'clock news. He thought about how he'd be remembered for posterity, and how that lasting image might sound. Jackson Cousins, a lifetime felon, finally and tragically meets his end in a shootout with local cops. Thankfully because of Sissy, he'd have a third option. He'd stand behind Sissy and use her as a human shield. Not only due to her size but also because of her status in the community, no one would want to be responsible for killing a God-loving woman. *Keep her in tow as long as she don't hinder you. If she does, release her. Same goes for Leroy, but he'll be released in another way, a more permanent fashion.*

"Knowing how far ain't gonna make it closer," Jackson said in response to Sissy's question after taking time to consider all of his options.

Leading the way, Jackson faced the initial wall of weeds. Some varieties of bushes armed themselves with sticky, sharp thrones that penetrated flesh, and as small as their pokers were, in masses they caused a great deal of discomfort. Luckily, Jackson had a machete in the bed of his Chevy, and now he used the blade to chop away portions of the wall of weeds to make a clear path. He hacked away at intertwining vines with one arm and held a rope bound to Leroy Blackman's wrists in the other. Leroy was stumbling around like a drunk, but he was making good progress, as if he was eager to get to where they were headed. Sissy took up the rear, following behind both Jackson and his prisoner, her huffing and puffing sounding like someone breathing behind a mask.

The dwindling light caused Jackson to realize it will be dark by the time they hacked through the natural barrier in order to reach the road on the other side. The path would lead them to Yazoo City, and from there he'd have to rely on Leroy to tell them which direction to take. Jackson wasn't too concerned with Leroy doing exactly as he was told. The Smith and Wesson had a way of intimidating men to do exactly what they were ordered. Jackson's real worry, one he had been keeping secret, was that he'd not be able to get a share (or the entire lot) of whatever bounty was to be collected behind the scheme Leroy and his partners, Lana (or Lorna) and Moody Johnson, were behind. Jackson wondered how much an insurance company would pay for the death of a wife. He believed without a doubt that the missing Shelly Cousins was dead. Collecting early on death insurance policies by assisting a loved one to an early grave was an old but proven way of increasing cash flow. It seemed to Jackson a bit more risky than profiting from the world's oldest profession or burglarizing a residence. But he wasn't the one who did the killing; he was just being the clever opportunist that he always had been. As he was concerned, it wasn't a crime to take advantage of a situation already in play.

Moody Johnson must be the big man in charge. Murdering a wife for the insurance money may have been Leroy's plan, but Jackson didn't see Leroy as the sort to have the intestinal fortitude to actually go through with something as violent as killing someone. Perhaps even the Reverend Perkins had been involved, and maybe he wanted a bigger piece of the insurance money pie; when he threatened Moody with whatever evidence he'd used in an attempt to blackmail his way into a larger cut, Moody had cut him out of the deal—along with what remained of the rest of his life. Jackson prided himself in being able to see the truth behind events; he could read people like a book, and the pages of Leroy Blackman life read like a child's nursery rhyme. *See Leroy get greedy. See Leroy want to collect insurance money on the death of his wife. See Leroy hire Moody Johnson to do the dirty work for him. See the Reverend Perkins join the conspiracy. See the preacher meet his creator sooner than he'd planned.* Jackson turned the mental page of his nursery rhyme. *See Jackson take advantage of all of them and reap the rewards.*

Jackson had believed it was an insurance policy scheme since Sissy had phoned him and provided him with the information concerning their missing sister, and the events that had followed Sissy hadn't presented any evidence to sway his previous thinking. He was sure that even someone as slow-witted to the nature of people as his sister must see the truth: Shelly was dead, and Leroy was cracking from the pressure. The thought of collecting some much-needed cash was the only solace in having to run from cops, hack his way through weeds, and get pricked in a hundred different places on his body.

4.

Andy's and Big Lou's progression came to an abrupt end at the same wall of interconnecting weeds and thick bush where Jackson and his group had realized they'd have to hoof it. Andy spotted a recent unnatural clearing, and he grabbed a flashlight and headed toward the mound of hacked weeds and vines lying on the ground.

Big Lou looked up to the gray sky, where even now he could see those final embers of light fading. It was like a man watching the final sparks of a protective fire flicker until the flames completely died, leaving him in alone in the dark and defenseless against the dangers surrounding him.

"It'll be dark soon," Big Lou said, stating an obvious and common fact. "I don't think it's a good idea to go in there, not in the dark. Not after Jackson Cousins." Big Lou stared into the weed-covered path much in the same manner he'd sat in the passenger's seat and peered into the darkness beneath Richard Blackman's porch, afraid one the hell hounds might crawl from within their dark, forbidding space; grab him by his ankles; and drag him into their lair.

"You have a choice, big fella. You can stay here and guard my Jeep, or for once in your life, you can do something for someone more than yourself. I don't care one way or the other. Whichever choice you make, can you do it without whining about it?" *Thank you. Couldn't have said it any better myself,* the voice of the Detective responded to Andy's berating of Big Lou.

Andy was surprised and a bit relieved, when he stepped into the thicket of weeds that Big Lou followed behind him. Andy could tell from his steps that he was still reluctant about this decision. But having the large, imposing figure of Big Lou as backup made Andy feel a bit more at ease in taking on Jackson, Leroy Blackman, and whoever else he may have to face. He'd radioed for backup, but there was no telling how long it would take for his deputies to drive to this isolated path and then trek though the bush behind him. But backup or not, he couldn't allow a murderer to escape. *Is that me, or is that the Detective talking? Either way, what does it matter if the words are true?* Andy thought.

5.

Jackson pushed Leroy, causing the man to stumble. Leroy's pace had been fine. Jackson had pushed merely because doing so made him feel good, sort of like when a boy caught a fly or ant and pulled off its wings or legs. The reason for doing so hadn't been because either insect had been a threat; the kid tortured the creature simply because the malicious action had brought him pleasure.

When darkness prevented him from seeing clearly, and when he couldn't manage to make out what a shape or form had been without being inches from it, Jackson decided to allow Leroy to take the lead so he could keep a better eye on him. Sissy still kept up the rear; she was too far back for Jackson to make out her form, but he could hear her labored breathing, and from the sound of her heavy inhales and exhales, she'd pass out from overexertion at any moment. The rough terrain worked in Sissy's favor, like a giant sloth whose body weight prevented it from bursts of speed but worked well in trampling or pushing aside obstacles impeding its forward movement. Sissy's size allowed her to swim through thick bush like the bulk of an African hippo allowed it to glide through water, as if the force of waves had less ability to restrain its progression than a gentle gust of wind.

Leroy stumbled from the push, but he didn't turn to protest because in a few more steps, he would be on the path where Mr. Moody Johnson resided. *Then we'll be seeing who'll be doing the pushing,* Leroy thought.

"Dear God," Sissy whispered between deep inhales and exhales of air. But her call to her heavenly father was not due to her discomfort, and it was not for her savior to remove the pain caused by prickly thrones or ease the burning in her lungs. Sissy's thoughts were not of her own current physical sufferings. Instead, she hoped that God had been with Shelly during whatever burdens she'd been forced to carry, those of metal and physical pain in which she'd labored when Leroy, that bastard of a man, had brought her out here to die among the weeds and dirt. *I hate you, Leroy Blackman. I hate, hate, hate!* Shelly screamed inside her head.

The trio of Jackson, Shelly Cousins, and Leroy Blackman had been trekking through dense foliage for nearly an hour. The path suddenly and unexpectedly cleared, and it was a shock to two members of the party. To the third, it was a sudden relief.

"Where is this? What is this place?" Jackson asked, staring around from one end to the other at the clearing in the path where there should not be an open space.

"We're here at the crossroads, at Mr. Moody's Johnson's residence while he's here on this green earth," Leroy gleefully responded. He spread his arms wide like he was a real estate agent showing a client the wonderful amenities of a luxurious home.

Leroy peered down toward the end of the path, where the road ended, and paths veering left and right could be seen. Standing at the end of the road, looking beautiful as ever, was Lana Monroe. She was wearing a skin-tight blue dress similar to the skin hugger she'd squeezed into when he'd first seen her sitting across the bar from him at Ruby's.

Leroy, you know you're completely insane, and you'll burn. You'll burn in hell's fires for what you've done, and for what you've become. Do you know that? His mama' voice was the only thing from his past that was capable of punching through the darkness from his past and reaching. Into his present thoughts.

Yeah, Mama. I've done gone nuts, and for what I've done, I'm for sure gonna burn. But I don't care, not one bit. I don't care anymore than you did when you didn't talk to me, when you abandoned me in all the ways a person can leave without physically removing herself from the same space she occupied with another person. Sure, mama, I'm gonna burn for what I've done. But you're burning for what you didn't do.

Leroy has this final face-to-face with his past, with the darkness and endless distance of his memories, from his current thoughts. He decided in that last moment that he'd never think of Mama or his past again, because he didn't have to. He could continue looking into the brightness of his trumpet, held between the fingers and palm of the most gorgeous woman he'd ever seen. He would wait here at the crossroads for Mr. Moody Johnson to come for him, to be that final judge and jury, and he'd welcome whatever punishment or praise there was.

Lana stretched out her arm, the one that held his trumpet. "Play it for me, Chocolate," she said.

Perhaps there is a hell on earth, Sissy thought as she pushed through the final barricade of bushes and made her way into the clearing. She noticed right away the area was made to resemble a crossroads. "Oh, God, protect me," she muttered as she brought her chubby fingers up to her chest, massaging the crucifix on a chain around her neck. "Shelly," she whispered not sure if she was calling for a living person or her sister's ghost. In this God-forbidden place, she was sure either may answer her call.

Sissy wasn't sure if she was thankful or saddened that Shelly didn't reply. Sadness was her dominant feeling, she decides, but she feared hearing or seeing a specter of her sister.

Her thoughts were interrupted by a more physical and immediate threat: Jackson's thundering voice, a vocalization as jarring to her senses as God's fury when he unleashed his lightning, followed by a earth-rumbling explosion of his power during a storm.

"I said, stop walking!" Jackson commanded as he pulls on the rope attached to Leroy's wrist, yanking at his catch as if he was pulling at a disobedient dog's collar.

Leroy was able to fight Jackson's pull for about twenty feet before the man's strength forced him to the ground. Still, Leroy had made it close enough to extend his arm and retrieve his horn from Lana's hands. He closed his eyes and placed his horn to his pursed lips. His hands shook like a man in need of moisture after a long, exhausting thirst. Shelly was dead. He may or may not be completely insane. He could see Lana clear as day. He may be the prisoner of Shelly's murderous brother and oversized sister, seeking revenge measured in pounds of her own weight. *How much revenge would that buy her?* Leroy thought.

Mr. Moody Johnson would be coming soon arriving to claim what he'd bargained for, what was owed. Mr. Moody Johnson, the man in black, the faceless man who could be anyone of his choosing. Mr. Moody Johnson, the seer and knower of all things, the demon waiting for men to succumb to their desires and sins. Leroy could forget about it all; he could have a moment of peace without thoughts of Shelly, Jackson, Sissy, Lana, and even Mr. Moody Johnson. He could have a few minutes—it didn't matter how long, but just a few minutes—with his horn. He could be that kid again, sitting on a chair that once belonged to his great-great-grandmother, in the middle of a cotton field with bud-laden cotton stalks bobbing over his head.

Jackson had thought to yank with enough force to bring Leroy not only to his knees but flat to his face. Then Jackson would walk up behind him, place a boot on the back of his head, and stomp on it until Leroy had to eat dirt just to take in air. But he'd been halted by what he now saw the man doing. Leroy's head lowered to his chin. His elbows were close together, and his hands were open, palms facing one other and spaced apart like he was holding something between them. But that wasn't as crazy as what Jackson witnessed next. Leroy pursed his lips like he was about to place a big wet one on the lips of a woman, but when he stared his smooching, he was only making it with the air. He put on a good show, like he was sucking face with a woman he had the hot's for.

Leroy's fingers moved like they had a mind of their own, gliding over the three valves of his trumpet at the precise moment breaths left his lungs and travelled through his horn. His air and finger placement combined to create perfects rhythms and harmony, manifesting in sounds emitting from the open end of his brass horn that perhaps exceeded the ability of Miles Dizzy and even his beloved Louis Armstrong.

"He's loony as a tune," Jackson said to Sissy as she walked up next to him, the rolls of her stomach still moving long after she'd stopped walking. Jackson decided he was going to introduce Leroy to his Smith and Wesson. He knew looking at the man that he'd gone over the deep end, and if there was some money to be had from an insurance policy on Shelly's life, Leroy was in no condition to convince an insurance agent that he was a mournful husband. Because of that, and because Jackson simply didn't like Leroy Blackman, Jackson was going to make him give Mr. Smith and Wesson a big, fat kiss on the lips—the sort of powerful ending that would literally blow off Leroy's head. The latter thought caused Jackson to laugh, and his joviality caused Sissy to become angry.

"The man done murdered your kin. I know you don't see me and Shelly like we are your family, but we're still kin, and don't nothing change that. Now you're laughing while she's somewhere near, probably beneath our very feet, rotting and being eaten by insects?" Sissy barreled past Jackson, brushing him aside as easily as she had those vines and weeds.

Leroy was deep into it. He'd fallen into that spell reached only a musician who had given all he had to his ability, part or all of his soul transported into an instrument, breathing life into an inanimate object the same as God had breathed life into man. He was creating life, a living manifestation of his inner self, a creation in his own likeness that was in possession of all his natures, until the creation acquired an ability to make a living manifestation of itself. Leroy's trumpet birthed his fear, doubts, love, hate, lost dreams, and purpose. The notes sounded like tears, laughter, pain, regret, and despair. Lastly, insanity came from his horn and entered his ears. They were prayers from his creation asking him, its father, for answers to questions it didn't even know how to ask, for forgiveness of sins and restoration of a wasted existence.

The slap on his face broke the spell, separating him from something like the bond between mother and child. Leroy lashed out like an angry beast, meaning to kill whatever had ripped that umbilical cord that had connected him and his horn.

Sissy went down with the first blow. The second cracked her skull, causing pieces of her brain to ooze from her head and fall to the earth. All this happened so quickly, too fast for even Jackson to pull at Leroy's restraints and drag him off his dying sister.

Leroy's next move, his madman burst, provided him with the strength of insanity. Inhuman endurance and physicality asserted itself in times of great mental suffering or overwhelming physical pain. The suddenness of Leroy's renewed and unexpected strength caught Jackson off balance, and he fell face down on the ground, eating with his breaths the same dirt he'd intended to force Leroy to consume.

"I'm gonna kill you!" Jackson yelled as he rose to his knees, his hands reaching for the rope that had been the restraint keeping his hostage under control.

Leroy made his way to the same dead tree where he'd first met Mr. Moody Johnson, where he'd decided to take him up on his bargain, trading immortality for purpose, for time to live what remained of his useless life in peace with a measure of joy. "Mr. Moody Johnson! Moody!" he yelled. "Come get me! Take me! I'm ready!"

"Okay then, Leroy. Okay. You gonna meet your Mr. Moody Johnson, you crazy son of a—" Jackson's insult was cut short as Leroy stood and faced him.

Leroy had placed on his head a black fedora. He'd put on an old, tattered black coat. Both the fedora and coat were much too large for his frame, but they were oddly fitting, as if he'd grown in stature just to fill out both hat and coat.

"Welcome to my home, Mr. Cousins."

The Colt .45's deadly end was pointed directly into the face of Leroy Blackman, and the key to its prison was on Jackson's index finger. All he needed to do was press down and open the door, freeing the power of Smith and Wesson's dangerous purpose. But Jackson hesitated. He blinked and tried to dismiss the thought, but it was there and needed to be said. He was not sure the deadly force, once released, would be enough to harm the man standing in front of him.

"Jackson, you don't mind me being familiar with you, do you? I'd like to believe we're friends, wouldn't you say? Jackson, would you sell your soul for it? Would you, boy?" the man in black asked.

6.

Following a trail of hacked vines and weeds had been difficult, and when night fell, seeing which of the vines had been hacked and which had fallen away on their own accord made it an even more arduous chore. The scream of a woman ahead and to the west provided Andy with which way to go; without having heard it, he'd have probably lost his chance of capturing his suspects.

"That way. It came from that way," Big Lou announced, pointing his finger in the direction of the screams like a birddog standing on three legs, one leg lifted upward and his body angled toward the area where he'd sensed or spotted game.

Andy emerged into the clearing followed closely by Big Lou, who seemed to have some inner courage that asserted itself at the sound of a woman in distress. Andy noticed a woman's body lying in the dirt, and he could see she wasn't moving. *Dead,* the voice of the Detective noted. Andy drew his revolver from its holster for the first time in eight years, other than when he removed it at the end of the day to return the weapon to a lockbox.

Big Lou had bolted past him and dropped to his knees next to the dead woman on the ground. Andy dismissed his feelings over the woman and the initial need to assist her; instead, he aimed his gun in the direction of who he believed to be Jackson Cousins. He thought he knew the other man, but he wasn't sure; the figure was in shape and size similar to Leroy, but after that physical likeness, the man could have been someone else. *He's the guy we saw in the interrogation room, the guy just behind the eyes and reach of Leroy Blackman, the guy who saw us too. .*

"Drop that gun, Jackson. Drop it now," Andy demanded. But already he could see in Jackson's eyes there was no way he was obeying that command.

Gunshots rang out at the same moment, so close together that folks near enough to have heard them couldn't say if it had been one or two shots fired. Neither Andy nor Jackson could say with any real convection which of them had gotten off the first shot. The debate over who had been quickest on the draw wouldn't matter in the future to Andy Collins, because it had been his aim that ended any real debate between duelers.

Andy himself did not notice the quick move as the man in black leaned down and retrieved the Colt .45 where it had fallen, along with Jackson Cousins, to the ground. Luckily for Andy, the Detective—that ever watchful and protective sixth sense, the other side of his personality—had noticed Leroy's advance.

Andy didn't shout out any forewarning to the man in black as he had to Jackson; he simply pulled the trigger. The bullet struck the man in black, causing the .45 to fly from his grip. But that didn't stop the man, and he lunged forward, running at Andy.

"Don't come any closer!" This time Andy did provide a warning, which the man in black ignored.

Andy fired again. The bullet went through the tattered material of a coat, and Andy knew it had entered near the chest of the approaching man—but it did not stop him. Andy fired again, then again, and again. All his shots were direct hits to the center mass of the crazed man in black.

"I am the man in black! I am Mr. Moody Johnson! I am forever! I live to torment the souls of men! I cannot be killed, not by you or anyone!" Andy unloaded, and the man in black kept coming. Andy's final shot was at point-blank, and as the bullet entered the man's chest, he fell over, his hands wrapped around Andy's neck with the force of a bear's grip.

Can't be, can't be. We unloaded on him. All direct hits! Said the Detective—or was it his own inner voice? Andy couldn't tell, and right now it didn't matter.

Andy passed out. The grip on his neck seemed inhuman, and he couldn't withstand the power. He didn't know what happened after he'd been choked to unconsciousness, and he relied later on details told to him by Big Lou.

The man in black stood and walked toward Big Lou. He walked up to him like those bullets had had no effect on him at all. He returned his black fedora to his head and dusted off the tattered black coat.

Big Lou later narrated, "I couldn't move, just stay there frozen, much as Sissy Cousins' dead body. What else would any other man have done when he came face-to-face with the physical manifestation of evil itself?"

Big Lou paused at this point in each telling of his story, of that day he came face-to-face with the devil at the crossroads. He'd stare into eyes of each man or woman gathered around him to hear his tale. Then after he was sure he had their full attention, he continued. "He walks up to me, no blood or nothing staining that black tattered clock of death. There was no pain heard in his voice, and although I couldn't see his eyes—and I'm thankful I hadn't, because if I had, I'd never sleep again—I was sure he was staring at me, past my eyes and into my soul. Then he asked me in a voice sounding like many voices at once, "Would you sell your soul for it?"

Before Big Lou could complete his telling, each time someone interrupted at this point, too eager to wait for Big Lou to offer his statement. "What did you tell him?" the impatient, curious listener would shout.

Lou would stare down, and with a serious and humble tone, he'd answer, "I said no—I wouldn't sell my soul."

When Andy finished writing his official report on what had happened at the crossroads, it wasn't filled with the fantasy and flair told in Big Lou's tale. He listed as many facts as he could recall, and he left the mystery of the story to Big Lou. He couldn't explain how Leroy Blackman had managed to withstand seven direct shots. But he knew there could be several reasons why a man may be able to do so. He simply reported the facts. At some point, Leroy began to lose his grip on reality, and that loss caused him to create a woman named Lana Monroe and a man whom Leroy had referred to as the man in black, or Mr. Moody Johnson. Leroy had built a home for this man to reside. He'd plowed away trees and grass to make a path in the middle of nowhere, a path leading to and going nowhere, ending at a fork in the path that also went no place, at least not in the minds of sane men. Then he'd murdered his wife, whose body Andy was certain was somewhere in the Mississippi. The body of Reverend Isiah Gerome Perkins was discovered buried in that crossroads where Leroy had lost his grip on sanity. Sissy Cousins had also lost her life, along with her half-brother Jackson. Last but not least was the bullet-riddled body of Leroy Blackman himself.

When all had been said and written of the story, the one conclusion Andy was certain of was that evil existed. If any man didn't believe him, he told him, "Stand in front of the mirror, and stare into the face of the thing on the other side of the glass. Look deep down into the darkness, into the lusting and wanting desires, and like Leroy Blackman, you'll be sure to discover your Mr. Moody Johnson, your man in black." When you do you can decide to either give into the darkness or fight with physical and mental endurance you can muster and hope it will be enough to escape those demons residing within.

The End

ABOUT THE AUTHOR

VINCENT EDMONDS EARNED a bachelor of arts degree in communication arts and human relations and a minor in journalism from Park University, Kansas City, Missouri. He lives in Stone Mountain, Georgia, and the United States Virgin Islands with his wife, Denise. This is Edmonds' debut novel.